HAVANA'S HELL

THE RATHE CHRONICLES BOOK 3

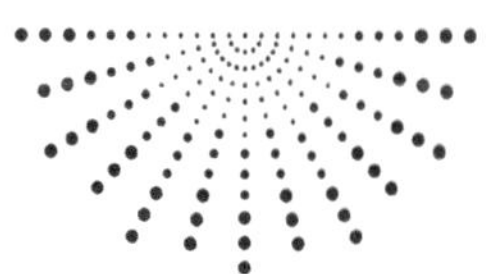

ALEXANDRA K. MARTIN

First Edition 2021,

Ebook: 978-0-6450508-2-0

Paperback: 978-0-6450508-7-5

Hardback: 978-0-6453856-9-4

Cover and Title Art: © DAZED Designs 2021

Editor: Melissa Plant

Formatter: © DAZED Designs 2021

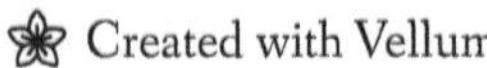

"Deep into that darkness peering, long I stood there, wondering, fearing, doubting, dreaming dreams no mortal ever dared to dream before."

— EDGAR ALLAN POE

FOREWARNING

Please be aware that I'm an Australian writer, therefore this book is written with British spelling in mind.

This is also a MF Fantasy/PNR novel, with adult content and is recommended for the mature audience. Please note that Havana has selective mutism from past trauma. It may contain some darker elements and possible triggers such as violence, captivity, PTSD, sexual harassment, implied childhood abuse and implied non-con. Please keep this warning in mind going forward and feel free to message me if you need extra information on any of the triggers. I'm happy to help.

Enter at your own risk...
*Insert evil laugh

Firstly, to my Grandparents for fighting all of my shadows when I didn't know how, and keeping me in the light of their love. You taught me how to be brave and to always believe in, and fight for myself.

"Put your shoulders back, and your head held high, because you count for something in this world." Eunice Margaret.

Secondly, to my babies (Even though you are definitely NOT allowed to read this yet!). Mama loves you so much and I promise to protect you forever and ever because hell hath no fury like your Mama pissed off. Ain't nothing gonna hurt you because no one is getting through me or your Daddy!

GLOSSARY

KINDRED S & KIDS

Summer

Blayze (Phoenix)

Salvatore (Dragon)

Reid (Alpha Wolf)

Baine (Omega Wolf)

Kids

- Meaghan (Human Female)
- Lawson (Human Male)

- Llewellyn (Human Female, Twin set A - Identical)
- Cheyenne (Human Female, Twin set A - Identical)
- Mina (Phoenix Female, Twin set B)
- Demetrius (Dragon Male, Twin set B)

Janice

Keneth (Grizzly Bear)

Anton (Grizzly Bear)

MHANU

Shifters

Phoenix (Rare and Powerful/ most feared shifter)

Dragons

- Dragon (fire Dragon/most powerful)
- Leviathan (Water Dragon)
- Drake (Earth Dragon/ no wings)

Wolf

Grizzly Bear

Shark

Cheetah

Griffin

Owl

Eagle

Panda

Sorcerers

Fae

Elves (Earth)
Fairy (Air)
Siren (Water)
Wielders (Fire)

Downworlders

Vampyre
Demon
Gremlin

DIVINE ORDER

Guardians

Angel
Valkyrie

Celestials

Catholic/Christian God
Norse Gods
Azraelle (Goddess of Rebirth)

PLACES

Rathe (Parallel world to Earth)

Threshold (Holding facility for human woman stolen by Rathe for reproductive purposes)

Downworld (World of darkness below and connected to both worlds)

Bermuda Triangle (Door between both worlds)

Marketplace

PROLOGUE

HAVANA

Please. Please. Please.

My thoughts are naught but pleas for mercy. My body is a trembling heap, stomach empty for days, with no energy to do anything but rock in a ball and pray for sleep to take me.

Janice told me she's coming back. I have to trust her; I have to hold on to that. I refuse to think of anything other than me going to her. I just want to go home. *Please, let me go home.*

Heavy footsteps boom down the stairs, and I brace myself. My fear is spiking so high and hard that I see stars, so I squeeze my eyes shut and just rock. Back and forth. Back and forth. Back and forth.

Why are there two people walking around?

I purposely breathe, trying not to panic as the footsteps pass the other girls and stop in front of my cage.

I have to remember what Blayze said. They will take me outside, and I need to ignore all the *men*. I shudder at the word. *Don't think about it.*

"So..." a smooth voice I've never heard before starts. "This is the female Blayze hopes to rescue, is it? This dirty little thing? Interesting." He's talking about me. *Oh God, why is he talking about me?*

A menacing laugh from the usual guard has me tensing up. "Yep, that piece of crap. Of all the females, *that's* the one they're waiting for."

No. This doesn't sound good. *Please, go away.*

With an impatient sigh, the new man says, "Alright, I'll take her. If he wants her, then I'm happy to ruin his plans. Smug fuck."

Wait. No. I start to rock harder as I hear the cage door unlock and squeak open.

Clomp. Clomp. Clomp.

Someone approaches me, but I'm too scared to open my eyes and just keep rocking. Back and forth. Back and forth.

"Open your eyes, pet," he demands, from too close to me. He must be squatting. "Now!" he shouts so loud my eyes snap open, and I clamber away with my back against the cold, smooth wall.

I quickly look at him and away. I can't bear to see men looking at me, I just can't bear it. *Stop it, stop it.*

"She never looks up at anyone, and I've never heard her utter a word, Sir. I think she might be slow. She doesn't even scream," the guard grunts with a laugh. "You sure you want that one?"

Leaning to the side to take me in more, he says with amusement, "She's not dumb. She's just smart enough to know that she *should* be scared. I can work with that, if anything, I prefer it. I'll have fun breaking this one down even more, and trust me, *I* can make her scream."

He reaches over and grabs my chin roughly as I shake all over so badly that my teeth chatter, forcing my face in his direction. "Listen to me, pet; I am Leon, and now you are *mine.*"

CHAPTER ONE

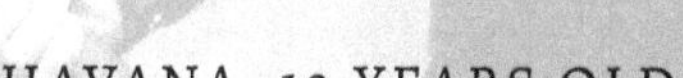

HAVANA, 12 YEARS OLD

My heavy eyes can't stay open anymore. It's late, and I'm so very tired. My blurry vision drifts between the TV in my room and my closed bedroom door, and the usual trepidation fills me. Lying in the dark is always the hardest part.

Slowly rising from my bed, I drag my feet across the rough, old, ratty carpet to my bedroom door. I take off the plastic bag filled with more plastic bags on the door handle and carefully place them all along the floor behind the wooden exit until I'm satisfied that they'll crinkle enough to wake me if *he* opens my door while I sleep.

With a deep shaky exhale, I switch off my TV and crawl back into bed, my eyes desperately seeking every inch of light they can find. The loud pounding in my chest and desperate gasping breaths fill my ears when all I want to do is hear beyond my walls.

I don't know why I'm so determined to be ready for when he comes back when I know there's nothing I can do about it. Nothing that will save me. But my need to be safe ignites every sense in my body, setting my once tired state alight with the heavy flames only deep fear can bring.

As the seconds turn into minutes, and minutes turn into hours, I soon see the sun begin to rise. The brand-new rays of the day ahead seep between my curtains, reminding me of another sleepless night. Reminding me of the constant state of fear I feel in my most vulnerable hours. While those beautiful rays represent hope, light, and peace to most people, to me, they are a stark sign of what I'll never know—freedom from fear, safety, and maybe even love.

Almost every morning I watch the sunrise because every night I'm too afraid to sleep. My school work is terrible because I'm always falling asleep in class. I can't learn anything new, and my teachers hate me for it, but I don't care. It doesn't matter if people like me. I have more important things to worry about than the opinions of privileged kids. I'm happy for them. I like to watch them play and laugh at lunchtime. It's how I know they're safe. I want them to be safe because nobody should have to go through what I do.

It's okay if the other kids try to bully me because I sleep too much at school, have no money, or don't have nice clothes. If that's the biggest thing they have to worry about, then that's okay by me.

Stretching my legs and yawning loud, I push myself out of bed, get into my uniform, and start to pack my school bag for the day. *I wonder which novel I'll take?* I skim my hand along my greatest loves and read their worn titles until I come to '*Flowers in the Attic*' by *Virginia Andrews*. Picking it up gingerly, I slide it into my bag with a smile.

I love this book. It's sad, but it's beautiful because no matter what happens, the girl is never alone. Being an only child has been the best and worst thing that has ever happened to me. I'm torn between being devastated that I have no brother or sister to help me and being so glad that no one else has to go through what I do. It's bitter sweet.

I get my stuff ready and leave the house as quietly as I can. The only time I'm really safe is after the sun rises because my daddy doesn't get up this early, ever.

Tiptoeing through the house, I leave through the front door and almost run to the bus stop. Every inch I get away from the house is a relief.

With a huff, I plop my bottom on the ground and sit on the grass next to the bus stop way earlier than I need to be. I think about my life and the heavy sadness that follows me everywhere, and my eyes burn with hot tears that I refuse to shed.

What did I ever do to deserve a daddy like this? I'm still only a child, but I must have done something wrong. Maybe if I had a mum, I'd be safe. Maybe if I was better? Maybe if I was quiet?

I'm just so tired.

CHAPTER TWO

HAVANA, PRESENT DAY

The world spins as I'm tipped upside down and thrown over somebody's large shoulder. I don't know whose, and I don't really care. After being lugged around by that terrible Bear-man for way too long, I've learned to shut my mouth and keep still. The memory of his immense hand almost squeezing the life out of me when I attempted to run is still fresh in my memory.

I keep my eyes squeezed tightly closed, unwilling to take in one more moment of this dreadful place. The saddest thing of all is that this isn't the worst place I've been in, not by a long shot.

"Take her straight to the sorcerer." I hear Leon order the man carrying me like a bag of potatoes. "He's waiting for us, and I want to get out of here before Blayze decides to check on her." His voice sneers at Blayze's name.

With a grunted affirmation, I'm carted up the stairs. The light brightening around us permeates through my closed lids, and as much as I wish that Janice will find me, my ability to hope died a long time ago. People say that hope is the one thing that never dies, but those people don't know what it's like to live in fear of it.

In a reality like mine, hope is dangerous. Hope is pain. Hope is the beginning of the end. Without hope, I can survive because I have nothing left that can be taken from me. You can't break me if there are no more pieces left to smash.

Hearing a heavy sigh to the side of me, I carefully open one eye and take a peek at the new man next to us. I've never seen him before, and if I didn't know any better, his dark eyes seem tinged with regret as he looks at me, pulling on his long dreadlocks over his shoulder.

"What are you waiting for, Twist?" Leon snaps behind me. "Open the fucking portal already."

The guy, who must be Twist, rolls his hands in front of him without a word. A deep magenta light licks through his fingers as he concentrates on them. The black of his eyes is swallowed by the same magenta hue. The pulsing light that could only be magic holds my full attention as he flicks it away, creating an oval hole the size of a small car sparkling with what looks like embers of red all around.

My gaze flicks back to Twist, and I find him looking at me ruefully. A small sad smile lines his thick lips, and he gives me a small nod filled with regret before turning and walking away, his leather hood falling from the back of his head with his quick strides, retreating as fast as he can.

Before I can think about what's happening, Leon and the ogre gripping me walk straight through the whirlwind of embers. Surprisingly, I don't burn, but a tingle washes over me instead. The bigger surprise, though, is when it pops shut like a bubble and the world around me is completely different. Instead of being in the same building, I now find myself outside, on a rocky ledge of desolate stone, with the turbulent sea crashing below me.

My senses are immediately assaulted. The cold, salty sea air blows across me, making my whole body shiver. The wind laps fiercely at my body, my dirty dress fluttering so hard I have to hold it in place. My head begins to thump heavily from the increased blood flow pushing on it from being upside down for so long.

With surprising speed and dexterity, Leon and his muscle fly across the open plain of rocks and bare ground towards a walled village ahead. The gates fly open as we approach, and my body jostles more with every movement, my headache growing more intense by the second.

"Get her into the tower," Leon exclaims excitedly with a clap of his hands. "The sooner we get her settled in, the better. Tell Verna she's here."

Verna? Maybe they have another girl here. I think to myself with a tinge of relief. The idea of being stuck in this place with only men is a terrifying prospect.

The large man carries me through a stone village and into what looks like a small castle at the edge of a large cliff that plummets to the torrential sea below. Without losing his breath at all, he climbs an excessive amount of stairs spiraling up a circular tower, stopping only when reaching the top before throwing open a large wooden door, revealing what I can only assume is a different type of cage.

My body is practically tossed onto a small, bare mattress on the floor of the sparse room. The movement is enough to make my stomach protest and head scream. The door slams behind the guy as he leaves me, startled and cold, on the rough springy mattress.

Squinting my eyes, I rub at my temple and look around the room the best that I can. My eyesight isn't very good, and my glasses were left behind at Summer's pack when I was taken.

The room is just like something out of an old movie. I'm obviously in the castle's turret, with circular walls and vertical, rectangular open windows. The only furniture adorning the room apart from the mattress is a small open toilet and sink.

Inhaling the sea air, I close my eyes and remind myself that I'm alive, and I can get through this. The scents mixed with the sound of the waves crashing from far below have a surprisingly calming effect on me, and I feel my breathing even out and my shoulders relaxing slightly.

Footsteps ascending sound from the stairwell, and I snap my eyes back open and push my body as far into the wall behind me as I can. Not ready to face Leon again so soon. Even though I know I'll never really be ready.

A light knock comes from the closed door before it slowly creaks open; a small head with short grey hair pokes around the side and peers into the room. An older lady enters with her hands held high in surrender, obviously to show me that she is no threat. Her petite frame and bony arms have me furrowing my brow in worry because this old lady looks ready to drop at any moment.

"Hello, sweet child," she starts, voice wavering slightly and eyes moist with unshed tears. "Don't be afraid. I'm not going to hurt you."

I know I should move towards her or say something, but my body is like a lead balloon, steadfast and heavy. My twenty years feel much longer than they should. Looking at this frail lady before me, I can't help but recognise that her outsides match my insides and the thought is tragic at best.

She steps carefully into the room, closing the door behind her, and all I can do is watch and wait. Having no idea how it can be that this woman is standing before me in a world that's meant to be filled with only men, minus the Valkyrie.

With a sigh, the woman lowers herself onto the end of my

mattress, her bones audibly protesting the movement. "Dear girl, I'm so sorry to see you here," she starts, with her head lowered sorrowfully. "As much as it's nice to see another female, I truly wish you weren't here."

Looking back at me, she takes in my huddled position, dirty body and clothes, and a look of fear that's no doubt plastered all over my face.

"My name is Verna, and I'm going to do everything I can to make things easier for you, but I have to be honest." Verna takes a shaky breath. "This isn't going to be easy. This place is filled with the worst kind of predators, but at least you will have the security of belonging to Leon because he won't share you with anyone else while he's trying to breed you."

Breed me? Of course, he wants to breed me. I leave my life with one monster just to belong to another. Nothing but a possession to be bred. When does my body become my own? When do I get a say on who gets to touch me? It feels like never. Just once, I want to know what it is like to be loved. To be touched with my consent.

I must have zoned out because Verna touches my hand, and I visibly jump at the contact. "You don't talk much, do you, child?" she asks me and I look away. "I'll stay in here with you as long as I can, but I have duties I need to attend to in the castle, or my son will punish me to the point that I won't be able to help you at all."

That gets my attention. "Son?" I ask quietly, my voice no more than a whisper.

Verna nods at me as I meet her dull brown eyes. "I birthed Leon. I'm afraid that I didn't have any say in his upbringing. Like you, I was taken for breeding, but unlike you, I was born here. My father and his father were old friends and some of the only Leviathans left in Rathe. When I was born, I was gifted to Shawn, Leon's dad and leader of the Leviathans, by my father to breed with when I came of age. I was only nine when I was brought here, like a lot of the female children of my time. My story is tragic, but not uncommon."

My breath catches, because as I look in this woman's eyes, I see the truth and the kind of pain that only people like us would know. At this moment, I know there's so much more to the story than she'll ever tell me.

"Unfortunately, my beast was bound as soon as I got here, and I never got the chance to become the Leviathan that I could have been. At least you don't have to be subjected to that. It's an awful feeling, losing half of who you are and feeling your soul cry out for the piece of you that's missing." Verna looks away with her eyes glazed over and miles away. Snapping out of it, she looks back at me with a weak smile. "Anyway... how about we get you cleaned up. I bet there's a pretty girl underneath all that filth."

I nod slightly and start pulling myself up. The desire to do something to please this sad lady pulls at me hard. If it means being less stinky, then I'm all for it. It's been way too long since I've been given a chance to wash myself properly, and I desperately need it.

Verna joins me and takes my hand gently, leading me over to the vintage looking sink, picking up and passing me a flannel. "Here you go. Wash yourself down, and I'll stand by the door and let you know if anybody is coming."

I carefully wipe myself down the best that I can, without having to take my dress off, still not overly comfortable here, regardless of Verna standing by because I don't actually know this woman. She is Leon's mother, after all.

Leaning over, I drink directly from the tap to quell my thirst. The cool fresh water feels amazing going down, and my stomach makes an appearance with a deep growl.

I look over my shoulder at Verna near the door with red

cheeks. It sounded like a beast was trying to let loose, but I'm ravenously hungry.

"Why don't I go and get you some new clothes and something to eat? They don't feed women very well here, though, I'm afraid. At least, not when we're not pregnant," Verna explains.

"Do you have more kids?" I ask, wondering how many other assholes are running around here.

With a small smile, Verna shakes her head. "Luckily, the Gods were merciful and made me barren after Leon. His birth was a difficult one, and I almost died bringing him into this world. The healer was able to save me, but my womb was destroyed and removed, much to Shawn's disgust because it made me no longer useful to him. By then, all the remaining females were either dead or taken." She sighs deeply and places her hand on the doorknob, opening it slightly. "He found another use for me, though. I'm here to keep up morale and supply to the needs of the masses. I would pick that any day over birthing another monster into this world."

"What do I do?" I ask quietly. Not sure what to say at her revelation.

Verna opens the door and says before she leaves, "Whatever you can to stay alive, my child."

Alone in the cold room again, I walk to one of the windows and look out at the vast ocean. A never-ending horizon, with a stunning sky of orange, pink, and purple as the sun slowly lowers. As time passes before me, my room lazily dons the dark shadows of the day passing, and the space around me becomes almost as black as my future seems to be.

CHAPTER THREE

LEON

Verna's pathetic form appears at the bottom of the tower stairwell after introducing herself to my new pet. I smirk at the satisfaction of the circle of life before me. My birth vessel, preparing the vessel that will birth my own offspring. It's good for her to learn her place as soon as possible. I don't have time to train it right now.

I watch her slink around from my hard wooden throne, enjoying her discomfort at having to be part of keeping my new breeder under control and following the rules. The old hag is only good for one thing usually, keeping my village satisfied. It's a shame that I couldn't get another pet while I was there, but I'll get a couple more at the next market. I can breed with them and lend them out once their bellies are full of my heirs.

She disappears into the kitchen, and an hour or so goes by

before she reappears again. Keeping to the walls, clearly trying to go unnoticed by anyone. Unfortunately for her, no one gets by me.

Pushing myself up, I stalk over to Verna as she heads back towards the stairwell with a bowl of food and intercept her before she gets a chance to go back up.

"Where do you think you're going?" I demand, knowing full well.

With her head down in submission, Verna replies, "I was going to feed Havana, Sir. I assumed you would want her body in good shape for breeding."

"I'll be taking that," I say as I snatch the bowl of plain white rice and grilled fish from her. "I'm heading that way shortly, anyway. I think she's had quite long enough to rest, don't you?"

Verna's head snaps up, concern for the pet lining her eyes. "But she just got here."

My eyes darken at her tone, and she immediately looks back down and apologises. "Watch your tone. I'd hate to have to punish you when I'm in need of your services to train my new breeder. Now," I continue, with no room for argument. Not that she would ever dare to argue with me. "The males have had a long day. See to your duties, pet; I don't want to see your face again tonight unless I ask to."

Turning on her heels, Verna scurries off like the rodent she is. Pathetic creature.

I look down at the half full bowl and scowl because I hate having to give a pet such a good meal. It seems like a waste of food. However, Verna is right, my pet is going to need proper nourishment to hold a child as strong as a Leviathan. For now, I'll allow it and can only hope that she is a fertile creature because my patience is already running thin.

I picture her small, curvy frame and my dick twitches with the excitement at getting balls deep inside her. I bet her cunt is tight, and the idea of filling it gets my feet moving faster as I take the stairs two at a time. I've waited for this for so long, and I can't believe it's finally within my grasp.

Stopping in front of the door, a dark grin spreads over my lips, and I take in a deep breath, not wanting to give away just how excited I really am. My hand grasps the door knob tightly, and I almost rip the door off as I thrust it open. *Calm down, or you'll break her.*

The room is pitch-black, but like most Mhanu, my vision is just as good in the dark as it is in the light. The haunting vision of my fragile pet standing at the open window, with her wild, frazzled hair blowing from the savage sea air, is enough to push my dick to its limits. The rock-hard appendage attempts to rip open my pants.

Her scent is old and even though I can see that she's cleaned herself, it's nowhere near good enough. She's going to need clean clothes too. That stupid, decrepit female forgot to clothe her in fresh garments. I'll just have to try to ignore the stench she's omitting.

"I brought you food, pet," I state, walking in and closing the door behind me as I watch her fold back in on herself. The sight has me sneering in delight. *Yes. You should be scared.* "Eat and then we breed. Don't take long. I'd like to get started as soon as possible."

My pet sucks in a breath and backs into the corner on top of her mattress and curls into a small ball. The idea that sitting like that will stop what's going to happen rips a deep, malicious laugh from me.

"I hope you don't actually think that's going to help you in any way," I say between laughs. "We can either do this the hard way or the easy way, and I've got to be honest, I hope you pick the hard way because I'd love to hear a scream pour from your usually silent mouth."

A small whimper escapes her and I move the rest of the way into the room, plopping down beside her on the grotesque old mattress, and thrust the bowl under her nose. "Now eat!"

Her tiny, delicate hand reaches out in the dark and takes the bowl from me, bringing it towards her face. Leaning over it, she picks up the spoon and begins to shovel the food into her mouth. I wonder how long it's been since she's eaten? I'll have to remember to supply her with extra food to keep her vessel healthy.

Unable to see her face clearly as it's always covered by her ridiculous hair, I lift it away from her and take in her features. She continues to eat as if I'm not here, and that's fine by me. If anything, I quite like that she doesn't speak; it saves me from listening to her blubber on or complain like I give a shit if she's happy.

Surprisingly, her features are quite pleasing to the eye. The complexion of her face, now that it's clean, is smooth in appearance, and her facial structures are well proportioned. She will make a fine breeder. Our offspring should be quite attractive with our combined genetics.

"Here's how it's going to work, pet," I begin, deciding it's best to explain what I'm expecting from her now that she's my property. "We will start our breeding today and every day after until you are successfully impregnated. Only then will you be required to please me when I'm in the mood, and if your pregnancy is going well, you will be required to bed my inner circle. I assure you that they will not use excessive force, as the wellbeing of our offspring is vital."

I pause to take in her expression, but it doesn't change even the slightest at my statement, and my eyebrow raises at her compliance. *Perhaps, this will be a better arrangement than I thought.*

"After the child is born, you will be required to take care of it until the age of eight. All the while, I will be expecting you to supply me with as many heirs as your body can handle. You will have a two-month reprieve after each birth to heal and prepare for the next one." Still, my new pet doesn't react in any way and I continue, pride at my choice of breeder growing. "When each child reaches the age of eight, they will be taken to start their own training. Any daughters will be strategically placed with allies for breeding, and any sons will be moved into the general quarters to begin warrior training."

I let go of her hair and lean back on the wall behind me. The breeder finishes her meal and stares down into the empty bowl, seemingly frozen in place. Taking it from her, I place it on the floor beside us and clap my hands together.

"Excellent work." I stand and swiftly start removing my clothes with an excitable grin. "I'll make sure you are fed three good meals a day, and you will make sure you keep hydrated at the tap." I nod behind me, forgetting that she can't see in the dark. "Now is when you take your dress off, breeder. Get into any position, I don't really care how we do it. I'm just looking forward to finally seeing what all the fuss is about. And don't worry, I'm in no hurry. I'll be here most of the night, filling you up as much as I can."

My last bit of clothing drops to the floor, and I stare down at her still form. "It's like that, is it? Okay." Bending over, I pull her chin up to look at me. "Hard way it is, then."

CHAPTER FOUR

HERMES

"This is a terrible fucking idea," Blayze grumbles under his breath, roughly rubbing his face with his hands as if to rub away what's going on. "Fuck it."

Standing up to his full height, which is still not as large as myself, but I'm taller than most, Blayze claps his hands together, garnering everyone's attention around us.

"This is a voluntary mission, which quite frankly could be a suicide mission, but if we don't try, I can guarantee a terrible outcome for Havana," Blayze starts explaining, his voice booming loud throughout the room. "I promised Summer we would do what we can to protect these females. While Janice here is safe," he points to the blonde female before him. "It has been confirmed that Leon has taken Havana straight from the marketplace via portal. We all know where Leon stands in regard to the human females, and it was agreed that we would understand that this could happen; I don't think it's right that we just sit by and do nothing when Havana could be in real jeopardy."

When Blayze and Leon went to the Gods about the human females being allowed freedom from Threshold, it was agreed that there would be certain threats to the females that were unclaimed Kindreds. While it seemed like a good idea at the time to give them the best chance at freedom and the ability to find their Kindreds, now that it's happening, the reality of the threat that the other faction is to them is hard to swallow; and none of us are willing to just sit by and watch it happen.

I would have met most, if not all, of the females while they were in Threshold because of being the facilities' chef, but I can't for the life of me remember anyone named Havana. Regardless, I have too much honour to leave this poor girl in the hands of that monster, Leon.

The Drake and Leviathan have always had a turbulent relationship with each other. While I was brought up with a heavy sense of honour, duty, and respect for the blessed Kindreds, the water Dragons don't have the same belief system. The lot of them believe human females are no better than pets and breeders with no rights whatsoever. The wars between the two branches of Dragons are historical and one of the main reasons why there is less than a handful of either of us left in existence. The fire Dragons are more of a split opinion, and were mostly wiped out from fighting each other. The wars, brought on because of the varying beliefs on the importance of humans, seem to be never ending.

Without a second thought, I stride towards Blayze, kneeling in front of him with my head bowed in respect. An unnecessary but meaningful gesture. I vow, "I volunteer my life in the search of the female Havana, and promise to do what I can to bring her to safety, in the event that she is without a Kindred."

I hear footsteps around me approach from all different directions as other males join me in kneeling with similar vows of service.

Blayze's large hand claps my shoulder, "Thank you, my friends. I wish I could be by your side for this mission, but as it is, I have been parted from my children for much too long, and my Phoenix is becoming aggravated at the separation."

Rising to my full height, I smile at my old friend, genuinely happy for his blessing. "Don't even worry about it. You have your own duty to fulfil, and I would never expect you to partake in this journey when you have young'uns to protect at home."

My heart fills with joy at the knowledge that there are two new babies in Rathe again. It has been too long since we've had one. How Leon and his faction don't worship human females alongside us is beyond my understanding. Without the grace of their love and devotion throughout the ages, we literally wouldn't exist. As far as I'm concerned, every single one of them is a Goddess in her own right.

"Hermes," Keneth greets with his usual laughing eyes and wide smile. "Let me introduce you to my Kindred, Janice." His arm pulls Janice in around her waist and squeezes tightly. Anton close behind, looking around the room with hypervigilant attention.

Holding my hand out to Janice, she takes it with a soft smile. "We've met," I answer. "How are you, dear? I hope these two buffoons are feeding you properly."

Janice shakes my hand with excited gusto and laughs musically. "I wish. Their meals aren't quite at your level, that's for sure."

"Hey. Hey. Hey," Anton intercepts with a frown. "I'll have

none of that, Sweets. You can't go around comparing other males to your Kindreds."

Keneth and Janice just laugh at him, making him frown even deeper, and Anton crosses his arms over his chest. "Oh, don't be like that," Janice coos, slipping out of Keneth's hold and wraps her arms around Anton's neck; his face immediately relaxes, and he looks down at her like she hangs the moon for him. "It's okay, my love, the only meat I want is yours and Chuckles'."

Anton reaches down and slaps her ass lightly, prompting a giggle out of Janice. "Cheeky female," he mutters before kissing her deeply. Keneth watches with crinkled happy eyes, and I can't help the longing that tightens in my chest at the public display of love and adoration between the three of them.

I'd like to say that one day that'll be me, but I'm a lot older than most of the males in this room, and if I've learned anything from the last couple of times we had females in Rathe, it's not to get my hopes up. Instead, I do whatever I can to protect those who find their Kindreds and the children they produce. If I can help them survive, I will.

While I live a completely hermit lifestyle in my home in the rocky mountains, I make sure to be available for any mission that protects the females and children. I've actually watched many of these males grow into the shifters they are today over the last few centuries. My mind is filled with memories; most of them, unfortunately, not good ones, hence why there are no females left. No matter how hard I try, at the end of the day, I don't seem to be able to protect them.

Lost in my thoughts, melancholy trickles up my spine, and I mentally shake my head and focus on the trio in front of me.

"Janice?" I ask. "How is it I don't remember a female called Havana? I thought I would have met all of you by now."

Looking uncomfortable, Janice tucks her hair behind her ears.

"Honestly, Havana gets anxiety around men and had some issues leaving her room for long periods of time. Summer and I found out that one of the other girls would take her bits of food to her room. I don't think she ever left her floor the entire time she was there. I'd never seen her before we were free of Threshold, either."

My eyebrows raise at that. "That's different." I play with my beard in thought. "If I'd known, I would've happily made up a tray to take to her room for each meal." Guilt fills me that I didn't notice, and there was probably a hungry female there the entire time.

Deciding that I'd better get a move on and start sorting out this rescue party, I smile and wish them luck in their future endeavours.

"My prayers grant the three of you a long, happy, and fertile life together. May the Gods be merciful," I say, with my palms facing upwards and giving a small bow. Janice's confused expression almost makes me laugh.

Keneth kisses her cheek with a chuckle. "It's the traditional blessing for newly claimed Kindreds. It's meant to bring good luck to all, and lots of babies."

"Speaking of babies," Anton growls in her ear from behind. "I think we should get started on that, don't you?"

"And with that personal comment, I'm going to take my leave," I add, stepping back. "Good luck Janice and congratulations again."

As I turn, Janice grabs my arm tightly. I look back at her and see her face is filled with worry. "Please bring her home, Hermes. She's not like other women. Something happened to her before she came here, and she's terrified of men and doesn't speak or look at them at all if she can help it. I'm really worried about her. She's not strong enough to go through this kind of thing. Please, please save her."

Hearing the fragility of the female we're meant to be rescuing has my blood boiling. The kind of horrific things that must have been done to her by a true monster for her to have such a visceral reaction to males must have been atrocious. The need to find her as soon as possible grows inside me, and I nod to Janice, promising that I'll do whatever it takes and keep in mind what she's said.

In the back of my mind, I make a note that she may not be happy to see a male such as myself taking her. I'm more than aware of how large and imposing I am. Of all the males here, my presence is most likely the fiercest. I am covered with tattoos, scars, and am quite literally built like a tree trunk. Rescuing her might be a bit more challenging when she sees me.

I move over to where the other males who vowed to help look for and rescue Havana are, nodding in greeting as I join them. "Thank you for joining me on this mission. As you all know, she is risky and may not have a good ending for everyone here. This is your last chance to back out," I say, waiting patiently. I look between the males before me and see no hesitation or regret. "Excellent."

"Does anyone here know where Leon's lair is?"

A feral grin lines my lips. "I do," I practically growl, the predator inside me a sinister reminder of what's coming and the desire to hunt, strong. "Get some sleep. We leave in four hours and won't be stopping till we get there."

"I've met her before," Baxter, a Cheetah Shifter, adds, "so I can point her out if I see her."

One of the Owl Shifters, Matthew, laughs and clasps Baxter's shoulder. "Dude, she's a female. I'm pretty sure we'll be able to figure out which one she is."

The males laugh and shout their excitement as they disperse, ready to face the battle ahead no matter what, and I'm proud to see such a brave group of males will be at my side.

Heading straight for the room I've leased while I'm in town, my fingers twitch with the need to sharpen my axes. I know I told the others to sleep, but there's no way I'll be able to get any tonight because all I can think is that there's a female out there in the evil clutches of Leon, and it makes me sick to my stomach.

I'm coming for you, little one. Just hold on 'till I get there.

CHAPTER FIVE

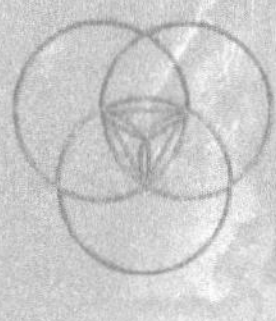

HAVANA

The last week or two has been a complete blur, the days drag into nights and hours seem to drift by. My mind has receded most of the time to my happy place, the special corner of my brain that allows me to pass through life with no awareness. While I'm not mentally here for anything even remotely unpleasant, my body is covered with signs of the things I've missed, making it impossible to be fully unaware.

My movements are halted and sore, and my body is never clean enough to wash away all the filth, no matter how hard I try. The only time I'm really here is when I eat, bathe at the sink, and wake up in the mornings with no memory of how I fell asleep.

The light of a new day streams through my window, and I stretch my aching body out, relieving some of the stiffness in my muscles from sleeping on this awful bedding.

Just as I sit up in bed, my bedroom door opens, and Verna

steps inside, her head down as usual and unable to make eye contact with me. Which actually works for me because I hate looking straight at people, even women.

"I've brought you breakfast, child," she explains, placing fresh bread and fruit beside my bed. "I thought we might take a walk outside today. It would be good for you to see some sun. You've been inside long enough."

Picking up an apple, I bite down on the sweet, crisp taste that melts in my mouth as I crunch. There's something simple, yet wonderful, about biting into fresh fruit. My mind floats on the random tangent of thought, everything else around me drifting away and unimportant.

Verna's gentle touch stills me. "I'm worried about you," she whispers, a shake in her voice. "Where do you go?"

With no intention or need to answer her, I simply resume the basic task of consuming the food before me. Her presence in the room barely registering.

Reaching down to eat more, I find the plate before me empty. Somehow I'd finished it all, but I don't remember doing it. I shrug to myself and go to lie back down, but Verna's hand wraps around the top of my arm, tugging at me.

I look up to find a scrunched-up, confused expression donning her fragile face. Her age is clearly defined in the lines telling her story. Every one of them is a key only she knows how to unlock. Everyone's journey is their own. While we might walk the similar roads, or have the same destination, our experiences are uniquely ours.

"Where are we going?" My voice comes out gravelly and quiet from not being used, and I wonder if I've always sounded that way.

Looking around, I see a descending stairwell before me and turning my head at the closed door at my rear; I can't quite figure out how I got on this side of it. My blackouts are getting worse, it seems.

Verna places her hand on my cheek and smiles weakly. "I'm so sorry that I can't help you, but I promise you're not alone." A lone tear streaks down the older woman's face, and I absently reach up and catch it with my finger.

"Don't cry," I breathe out. "Everything will be okay."

I turn away and walk down the stairs until I reach the bottom. It opens up into a large stone room with a vast array of men walking around and going about their business. Verna grabs my wrist and drags me away from the scene, pulling me to move faster.

"You don't want to linger around these men longer than you have to. Trust me," she explains as we head outside and towards the cliff edge. "Let's go and look at the sea. It's calm today, and the wind is softer than usual."

With the sun beating down on my skin, I let her take me to a bench facing the ocean and sit carefully. My head falls back, and my eyes close as I let the warmth seep into my skin, a warmth I desperately needed.

I hear Verna's light footsteps as she surrounds me, pulling my hair back from my face and gently stroking my head. She pulls my hair tighter, and I feel her small hands tie my hair up in some kind of band.

Never opening my eyes, I keep still and bask in the welcome rays of the day as she takes care of me. First tying my hair back and then lightly massaging my shoulders, humming a gentle, unfamiliar tune. My body loosens up, and I relax into the moment, focusing on the sound of lapping waves below us, and for a moment, I pretend that I'm at the beach with my long-lost mother. Just the way my life should have been.

My mum's boisterous laugh tickles at my memory, her face

no more than a blurry vision. My last good memory of her is when we were at the park, and she was pushing me on the swing.

Her warm brown skin, darker than my own light-brown hue, as she would hold my hand, and we'd walk along together laughing. The vibrant green grass of New Zealand is always beautiful and full of life. When we would sit together, she made me pretty rings of flowers that she picked from the ground and placed on my head like a crown. I was her little princess, and she was my queen.

I miss her every day, and sometimes when my mind can't deal with my reality anymore, she will visit me, and I will be a child laughing in her arms once again. Mum is my angel even now, protecting me from everything, even myself. I know that if she were here that my life would be different, but no matter what happens, nobody can take away my memories of her.

"If it isn't Leon's new pet," a deep voice says to the side of me. Verna's hands are still on my shoulders, and I instantly feel her body tense. "I'm looking forward to taking you for a ride, little one. Leon says you're tight and compliant, just the way I like it. Unlike this shrivelled old thing behind you."

My body remains completely still, and I make no move to react in any way. I learned a long time ago that it's better to be still and quiet, because they're just looking for a reason to make things worse than they are.

The male grunts and asks Verna, "Is she slow?"

"No sir," Verna clears her throat, clearly afraid of the man. "She just has trouble communicating."

He scoffs, "Sounds like she's slow to me. Hopefully, it doesn't affect her breeding quality."

Hot breath fans my face as he no doubt leans over me. A calloused hand rubs up from my knee to my thigh.

"Please, Sir," Verna pleads quietly. "Leon won't like you touching her until she's impregnated."

He just laughs and licks my cheek, as his hand rises dangerously close to where it shouldn't, and I feel the darkness trickle in, pulling me away from the here and now.

A booming voice behind me rips me back to the present. "No. He will not." Leon's voice has an angry growl to it. "You better have a good reason for touching my breeder without my permission, Virgil."

My head falls forward again, and I open my eyes to see Leon glaring at a man almost twice his size, but clearly afraid of him.

"Sir, I was just seeing what she felt like," the large man defends. "I wouldn't have fucked her, I swear. I know the rules. I just figured it couldn't hurt to see what she felt like compared to Verna. It's been a long time since she was young enough to feel tight."

Leon shoves his finger into the other guy's chest. "Let me make it very clear," his words filter through ground teeth, his cheeks reddening with fury. "No one is to lay one finger on her until she is pregnant, and I am through with having her all to myself. She is my property, and if I see you near her again before that time, you will not be one of the males lucky enough to partake in her cunt at all."

His vile language reminds me of my father, and it makes me sick. I'm not sure which is worse between them anymore. I'm lying to myself because Leon isn't even half the monster my dad was. Leon is just a bad guy doing bad things, but my father... he was meant to protect me, not be the thing I needed protection from.

"Is she empty again?" I hear Leon ask Verna with disgust in his voice.

I blink several times and look around, wondering how long I've been here.

"If I may say so, sir," Verna starts nervously, "I don't believe she is doing very well with the arrangement. It seems she is disappearing further and further into herself, and I fear that one day she may not come back at all."

Leon scoffs, "Who cares, as long as her pussy does its job. She doesn't need to be mentally active to bear me young. If anything, it works to my benefit because I don't have to deal with her shit." He pats my knee. "It would be better if she were a good lay, though. Oh well, I'll be seeing you later, pet. Get her back inside, feed her, and get her clean for me. My dick's hard, and I'll be using her a bit earlier than normal, I think."

He leaves us alone, quietly together, by the edge of the cliff. I turn my head to look at the large drop only a few feet from where we are, and I can't help but wonder if I'll fly. Maybe if I do a run-up, I'll fly over the edge and into a quiet place that I don't ever have to leave. A place of peace where no one can hurt me anymore.

"No!" Verna snaps at me, holding my face between her hands tightly. So close to me that she's blocking my view.

I look down at my feet. I'm standing and Verna is in my way.

"There will be no flying for you," she whispers, her words trembling. "We're going back inside now, child. I shouldn't have bought you over here. I don't know what I was thinking."

Did I say that out loud? Was I really going to try to fly? I can't quite remember. "I'm tired," I rasp, suddenly exhausted.

"I know, darling. I know." Taking my hand in hers, Verna pulls me away from the edge and step by step I get closer to another night of darkness; of dreams that disappear.

Back in my room while waiting for Verna to bring me my next meal, I gaze longingly at the sky through my window, and whisper to the Gods that apparently listen here, "Why?"

CHAPTER SIX

HAVANA

"You shouldn't have gotten between us," I voice quietly as I clean Verna's split eyebrow, dabbing the blood away with a clean towel I was saving for washing up later. "I don't want you to get hurt."

I know Verna was just trying to help when Leon came in earlier, throwing me down onto the mattress as I was eating my lunch with her. With my head getting pushed into the bed, I was starting to fade out when I was snapped out of it by a loud smacking noise and Verna's cry of pain.

Turning my head, I looked up to see Leon standing over her crumpled form on the floor.

"Stay out of my way, you old bitch," Leon snarls with fury. "You ever grab me like that again, and I'll skin you alive, you useless piece of shit."

It worked though, as he tore out of the room in a rage,

slamming the door against the wall in his retreat and making me jump. The stomping of his heavy boots echoing down the stairwell until he reached the landing. With the room silent once more, I carefully get up and crawl over to Verna and her tear-stained cheeks, a trickle of blood weeping down her face.

Her frail fingers touch my hand as I wipe her down tenderly, trying not to hurt her any more than she already does. "Sweet girl, I couldn't just sit there and watch him do that to you in front of me. I know better, but I just reacted without thinking about it, and I'm so sorry that this is your life and that I birthed that monster. There's nothing redeeming about that boy."

Verna shakes her head sadly, and her hand drops back down in defeat. I'm sure she wants to save me as much as I want to save her. We are together in this hell, after all.

"What was your mother like?" Verna asks me suddenly with sad eyes. "I always wanted to be a good mother, but that choice was taken from me the moment Leon was born. I was only allowed to breastfeed him, and when he was one, they took that away too. He was taken to stay with his father until he was eight and then was placed in with the warriors to learn how to be vicious. I never had a chance to do the right thing with him. If I even dared try to talk to him, I was beaten and my bones were broken so many times that after a while they stopped growing back properly, and I live in constant pain. I wanted so much for him. Please tell me your mother cared for you the way a child should be cared for."

Turning my head away, I look out the window. "From what I can remember of my mum, she loved me, but she died when I was pretty young and then..." I taper off, unwilling to think about my life after she left me.

I can almost smell the rain that soaked me that day. Standing outside crying and watching the paramedics gurney her away, her body still and cold. My screams of *Mama* still echo in my mind, the sound foreign to my own ears and so heart-wrenching that it brought the neighbours out of their homes to stare at me standing in the middle of the street, during one of the most fierce storms I've ever seen. Maybe it's because with each crack of lightning, my small heart cracked a little more.

My dad eventually scooped me up and carried me inside, telling me to shut up and stop making a scene. He wrenched my shivering body through the door as the ambulance disappeared from view down the narrow street. In my young four-year-old heart, I knew deep down that I'd never see my mummy again, and it broke me. No matter how hard I screamed, cried, and begged, she never came back, and my life was never the same again.

"Havana?" Verna queries softly, dragging me from my devastating memory. "It's okay if you don't want to talk about it. You don't have to go back there. Stay with me. You don't need to hide away right now. I'm with you."

Inhaling deeply, I let the memory drift away and focus on the stone walls around me, grounding myself to reality for Verna. I hear the fear in her voice when she knows I'm fading away. I think she's worried that one day I might not come back and honestly, I'd be okay with that. Every moment of every day, I feel exhausted.

"Shall we finish our lunch, child?" Verna says, grabbing my hand. She walks us back over to the mattress, and we sit down, picking up our previously discarded sandwiches, and start eating them again in comfortable silence. I'm glad I met Verna here; it's nice having a friendly face that I can relax with. I just wish we'd met under different circumstances. She's the kind of mum anyone would be lucky to have, and Leon has no idea how lucky he is to have her.

I swallow another bite and look sideways at Verna. "I think you would have been a great mum. Thank you for caring for me."

Looking back down, I continue eating, ignoring the way Verna sucked in her breath before releasing a sob.

"Th-thank you," Verna stutters, sniffing her nose. "If I got to choose to have a daughter, I would choose you, beautiful girl."

* * *

HERMES

Heading up the group, we move across the land quickly in our Shifter forms, except for the Siren, Neville, who rides on my back. The Owls, Matthew and Scooby, fly above us, while Baxter runs on my left in Cheetah form, Derryn on my right in Wolf form, and Sebastian holds the rear as a Panther.

As we approach Leon's territory, I gesture for the group to slow down, not wanting to alert them to our oncoming approach. The element of surprise will hopefully benefit us if we can keep it.

Neville slides off my back with his large duffel bag filled with our clothes and weapons, and starts unpacking for us as we all shift back into our human selves.

Matthew and I approach him to gather our belongings, and I grasp my axes with a twisted smile, ready to fuck some shit up. The others choose to fight as their beasts, but I can't pass up an opportunity to use my babies.

Scooby shifts quickly and says, "I'm going to fly over the village and see if I can spot where they're keeping her. If we're lucky, I might be able to carry her out if she's not too big."

An unexpected laugh pops out of Baxter as he shifts as well. "Trust me, you can carry her. She's the smallest human I've ever seen. I swear she's almost the size of a child, especially with her personality."

"What does that mean?" I demand.

Baxter puts his hands up. "Calm down, big guy. I'm just saying that she's not like the others I've been around. She doesn't speak, and she's always looking down. My Cheetah hates it. It makes me really uncomfortable, like I need to defend her all the time. There's something about her that seems like she's being threatened all the time. It keeps me on edge."

"That doesn't sound good," Matthew says warily, and I nod in agreement.

Before shifting back, Baxter says with a shrug, "You'll see for yourself soon enough."

Choosing not to linger on what that means for her upbringing, I order the others to follow me to higher ground, where we'll have a direct line of sight with the village.

Scooby takes off, and we begin our ascent, careful to keep our heads down and feet quiet in case there's someone nearby that could hear us.

As we get into position, crawling on our stomachs in beast and man form, I peek over the top of a rock and take in the bustling village below me, and it's obvious that they haven't noticed us lingering nearby.

We watch carefully at the guards' patterns and Leon coming and going from the castle on the edge of the cliff. Because it's early in the morning, everyone seems to be getting into their daily chores, and I'm surprised to see an elderly lady hobbling through the village every now and then. It's clear that she's been here for a very long time and may not have all that many years left.

"Those fuckers," Matthew growls beside me as he watches the old female being knocked down by one of the males on purpose for his amusement. The shifters at our side huff in agreement. None of us happy about finding out they've probably been mistreating this female all these years.

Scooby swoops down in the trees behind us and then carefully crawls up to where we're hiding and lying low. "I think I found her," he whispers. "She's in that tower in front of us. Right at the top, but she seems to be sleeping, and there are guards everywhere, so I can't get any closer without them seeing me. I think I can probably get to her tonight if you guys take out the guards at the back of the building."

"Good plan. For now, we'll keep watch and see what happens," I agree, wanting to get this done as soon as possible, but knowing I can't rush it. "Cats, tonight, why don't the two of you and Neville stay close to the bottom of the hill in case we need backup?" A big black paw smacks the back of my head, and Matthew laughs quietly at Sebastian's grumpiness with me calling him a cat. "Sorry, I couldn't help it," I laugh. "Scooby, because you know the lay of the land best by now, you keep an eye out for anyone getting suspicious and Matthew, can you fly in the window and convince Havana to follow you out to the back door?"

With a single nod, Scooby agrees, and Matthew replies, "It's as good as done."

Fury builds between us, and we continue to watch as Leon disappears into the tower before us. Sitting still, when I know he's climbing those stairs to the poor girl above, feels almost impossible, and I have to drop my head onto the rock below me and breathe in and out. Trying with all of my might not to think about what he could want with her, and praying he leaves her alone.

"I hate this shit," Neville grumbles at my left, obviously as frustrated as I am about having to sit here and do nothing.

Scooby sucks in his breath before saying. "There she is."

My head snaps up, and it feels like a heavy boot smashes into my chest the moment I see the fragile beauty standing at the windowsill with her eyes closed and the wind whipping her wild, curly, black locks around her face. Her perfect brown eyes pop open, and she stares longingly out towards the sea, and my heart stops at the same time my beast roars in my head; *Mine.*

All the oxygen leaves my lungs, and I unconsciously sit up, unable to look away from the tiny creature that is, without a doubt, my Kindred. How on earth Anton didn't figure out Janice was his immediately is beyond me because as I stare at Havana, my heart sings, and I ache for her.

"Lie down," Matthew gasps, grabbing my fur cover and pulling me back to the cold stone below me. "Are you crazy? They'll see you sitting up like that. What's wrong with you?"

I shake my head and rub my eyes. "Nothing. Sorry," I defend, not wanting to admit it to them right now until I can wrap my head around it. I was sure that I'd never find a Kindred of my own.

Shock, mixed with excitement and dread, fills me. On one hand, I'm ecstatic, but on the other, Leon is near her, and I can't do anything about it. *Fuck!* I need to stay calm and trust that everything's going to be alright. She's lasted almost three weeks here so far. I'm sure she can get through a couple more hours.

She has to.

CHAPTER SEVEN

LEON

Still pissed off about yesterday, I stomp up the stairs to get to Havana; the test clasped in my closed fist. I'm not in the mood for breeding right now, but it's about time I start checking to see if my efforts to impregnate her are working or not.

I smack the door open and watch with glee as the little bitch jumps at the sound. At least I get the satisfaction of watching her tremble in fear. There's nothing quite like it. Unfortunately, I don't get to enjoy that as often as I'd like to because her mind seems to disappear whenever I get close to her, and she's as limp and empty as a soggy noodle. She's obviously mentally challenged in some way. I can't even get a flinch out of her if I pinch or smack her. It's like she's dead inside, so I'll enjoy these little wins whenever I can get them.

"Come here, pet," I demand, not in the mood for her tepid personality. "Hurry up."

Jumping at my command, she meanders over to me with her head down, as usual. I grab her arm and prick it unnecessarily hard with the little device the healer gave me last week. A tiny squeak pops out of her, making me smirk. *Didn't expect that, did you?*

I let her arm go and lean on the door jamb. "Fuck off, I'm done with you." I shoo her away with my hand, and she scurries into the corner like the rodent she is.

To my absolute delight, the test turns green between my fingers and a loud "*Whoop*" tears from my lips. Oh, my Gods. I've done it; she's pregnant. I look over at her with the first genuine smile I've had in forever.

"Well done, pet," I compliment. "Our feats have been a success. I will increase your food quantity and won't have to touch your filthy body unless I want to now. I might even let you down once a week to use my bathroom facilities. You sure as hell could use it; you fucking stink."

The breeder's face rises, eyes swimming in fear and shock, and I fucking love it. If she didn't know she belonged to me before, she sure as fuck does now.

I push my body off the door jamb, leaving the room. I run almost directly into Verna. *What a disgusting old hag.* "Good news, wench," I smirk at her. "The procreation attempts were a success."

I get a sick satisfaction watching her face drop and push past her down to the landing. I grab one of my generals. "Organise a party for tonight. I'm having a baby."

The roars of applause around me fill me with pride. I will fill this land with Leviathan yet, and we'll take control before the other fools know what to do.

* * *

HAVANA

Holy shit!

I can't be pregnant already, can I?

My hand slides over my flat belly, and my eyes widen at the possibility. That was so fast. I'm not sure how I feel about this.

I'm torn between the absolute terror beating against my chest cavity, making me want to bend over and vomit, because I can't give that monster a child, my child; and then there's the undeniable relief at the idea of Leon leaving me alone for now. Maybe I'll be able to sleep through the night without the fear that he'll wake me up?

My door opens and a visibly pale Verna stumbles into the room, her eyes immediately dropping to my stomach, and I know she knows. Her own inner battle at play.

"Oh, child," she sobs, rushing to me and embracing me with everything she has. Tears that I desperately wanted to avoid slip free from my eyes and roll down my cheeks unchecked. The sound of Verna's sobs, increasing my own; the reality of what it means to be pregnant by him, seeping in.

My arms wrap around her as we both drop to the floor where we are and hold each other tight; the sounds of our combined sorrow filling the hollow room around us, almost as if it cries along with us.

"What do I do now?" I sob in her ear, my shoulders shaking violently with my pain.

Verna's head shakes from side to side. "I don't know, but you're not alone, and I'll do everything I can to keep this baby with you as long as possible."

I lean back and wipe my eyes with my sleeve, trying to regain control over my erratic breathing. "Will he leave me alone now?" I ask, a desperate edge to my small voice.

"I truly hope so, but I wouldn't count on it," she tells me honestly, and I appreciate that she's not just telling me what I want to hear because that doesn't help anybody, least of all me.

* * *

As THE NIGHT APPROACHES, sounds of joy and celebration teeter up through my windows. No doubt a party to honour Leon's heir. I'd shake my head at the preposterous notion if I wasn't feeling so despondent.

Verna stays sitting with me quietly, understanding my desire for silence. The night slowly closes in, but neither of us makes a move to light a candle or make any movement, really.

"I suppose I should get you some dinner," Verna says suddenly in the dark. "I'm sorry I didn't get it earlier. For some reason, I didn't realise how late it was until we were sitting in the darkness."

I reach over and pat her hand. "It's okay. I'm not hungry." My stomach has been swirling since I found out, and I can't imagine keeping any food down right now.

"You need to think of the babe, Havana," she reasons, pulling herself up. "I know the last thing you'll feel like right now is food, but you have to take care of yourself more than ever. A part of parenting that you can take charge of is having a healthy baby. Technically, that's my grand baby in there, and the least I can do is make sure it's fed well."

Knowing she's right, I stand up beside her without any disagreement. I might not be able to control much here, but I decide at this moment to do everything that I can for this little life inside me.

It's okay, my cherished love. Mummy's got you.

"You're right," I state, pulling my shoulders back and deciding that I need to be stronger now than I ever have been before. I will be everything I can that I didn't get as a child. "Whatever you can do to help me would be really appreciated. Thank you."

Verna pulls me into another hug and pats my back. "Thatta girl. We've got this."

She lights the lamp by the door, and turns towards me with a smile, both our eyes long since cried out. Verna's hand freezes on the door handle, and her head tilts in question. "Do you hear that?" she asks quietly.

Paying attention, I focus on the sounds around us and almost squeal as a giant white Owl swoops in through the window, resting on the sill before hopping down to the ground between Verna and me.

Verna gasps when the Owl shocks the hell out of the two of us, shifting before our eyes into a tall, naked, pale, red-headed man. My eyes almost bug out of my head, and I rush to the back of the room, pushing my back into the wall, and sliding down into the foetal position.

My heart beats furiously in my chest at the incoming attack of this unknown man, and I cling to my stomach, desperate to cover my unborn child from the looming threat. I pant furiously, unable to catch my breath as panic overcomes me.

"Shh, shh. It's okay," a man's worried voice says quietly over me, but all I can think about is my baby and his proximity. "I'm not going to hurt you. I'm from the other faction, and I've come to rescue you. What's wrong with her?" he asks Verna.

Verna's hands slide over my back, making me jump. "Child, please calm down." Her soft voice flows over me and I try to focus on what she's saying to me. "I've got you. You can trust him, the other faction is safe for you."

Leaning into her, I let myself relax a little, trying to tell myself that if Verna's not scared, then it must be okay, but it's easier said than done. A whimper escapes my lips, and I hear the man curse quietly in the background.

"I'm sorry, but we need to go before they figure out what's going on," the man almost whispers.

"I don't know who you are, but I'm trusting you," Verna says to the Owl-man, then lifts my face to look at her with a stern face. "It's time for you to get your shit together now, Havana. I know you're scared, but you have priorities now, and that means getting the hell out of here," Verna whispers to me. "Now get up and let's go. We're getting you out of here."

I suck in a deep breath and nod once, letting her pull me to my feet, keeping my head down and away from the man in the room. I don't know or trust this person.

"Whatever you do, don't touch her without warning," Verna tells the man. "She doesn't talk much and is terrified. Do you understand?" I'm momentarily stunned by the steel in Verna's voice, because I'm so used to her being almost as submissive as I am.

"Yes, ma'am," the guy agrees, and I relax a little more, happy that I don't have to worry about him groping me. "My name's Matthew, and I need you to stay close behind me and get ready to run if I tell you. Hopefully, we'll get out of here unnoticed because for some reason there seems to be some kind of celebration going on and everyone's pretty drunk already. Regardless, it's important for you to stay as quiet as you can. We're going out the back door, where others are waiting to take you to a safe location," he explains carefully, but I remain clinging to Verna's side. She agrees for the both of us, and Matthew opens the bedroom door.

Quickly and quietly, we race down the stairs, the loud sounds of the party in full swing outside, hiding any sound of our retreat. Verna holds my hand tight, and she moves faster than I thought she was even capable of because of her age and previous injuries.

As we get to the bottom stairs, Verna grabs a hold of the man's wrist ahead of us, directing him to a different direction than he was about to turn, and he nods, letting her move ahead of him to a door at the end of the corridor.

"Go straight through here and turn left, then right," she explains quietly to Matthew. "It'll take you out the back door. There's usually two guards out there at all times, though, so be careful."

Matthew nods and then looks between the two of us with a knowing look. "You're not coming, are you?" he asks her, and my breath catches in my throat, my head snapping up to her face.

She smiles at me and strokes my cheek softly. "No. I'm sorry, my child. I need you to be safe and get as far away from here as you can. I will stay guard and keep them from finding out where you are for as long as I can."

I reach out and pull her into me, my body suddenly overtaken with trembling limbs. "Please, no," I whisper in her ear.

"Shh, now," Verna coos, releasing our hug and stepping back. "Stay with Matthew and trust them. They'll keep you safe, I promise. Be safe, my dear." She turns to the man beside her. "I'm trusting you with her life. You will not let me down," she demands, with her chin high and her eyes and mouth tight.

Matthew bows deeply and kisses her hand. "I will not let you down, female. Havana will be safe with us. I put her life ahead of my own from this moment forward."

With burning eyes, I watch as Verna opens the door, pushing me and Matthew inside. "Live, love, and be free," she says before closing the door in my face, leaving me shaking and filled with pain.

"We need to go," Matthew says. "I'm going to take your hand now, female. Please, trust me."

I don't fight him as he grabs my hand and pulls me through the next few doors until we dash outside. Looking at my feet, there are two men slain, one of the bodies is missing a head, and I take a step back, pulling on Matthew's hand.

"It's alright, female. They're just the bad guys," he says, trying to calm me down. He pulls me harder. "Come on. This is Hermes and Derryn. They're friends of mine, and they won't hurt you, I promise."

Moving forward with him again, I walk as fast as I can until I make the mistake of looking up and see the biggest, scariest man I've ever seen in my life, and his tattooed face is covered in the blood of the guards, some of it dripping off his thick beard.

Oh my God, I'm going to die.

CHAPTER EIGHT

HERMES

Nothing could prepare me for the avalanche of emotions that overtakes me at the sight of the tiny, terrified creature before me. Her fear permeates the air around us at the bloodied vision of me post slaughter of the village guards. There's nothing I can do about how I look right now, and I'm furious with myself for not thinking about how I'd look to her.

Havana's even smaller than I had originally assumed from what I saw through the window earlier, and the urge to pick her up and carry her away from the threat that this place represents to her is fierce. My beast, however, has a whole different idea. The thrashing need to rip Leon to shreds, almost too strong to resist.

Derryn, apparently sensing my inner conflict, steps in front of me with one hand up, while passing Matthew some pants with the other. He tells Havana, "Lass, I ken we look mighty scary right now, but I swear, we're here to help."

Matthew quickly pulls his pants up and grabs Havana's hand again, and the sight of him touching her has me growling low with menace at him. He cocks an eyebrow at me and shakes his head before whispering to the frozen Havana. "We have to go. You can freak out later. They won't hurt you."

She whimpers quietly as Matthew pulls her away from the building as quickly as he can. While I logically understand why he's doing it, seeing him touching her and dragging her away from me has me clenching my teeth and tightening my grip on my axes. *I need to get a hold of myself.*

I decided earlier not to let the others know about Havana being my Kindred. I'm a very private male, and I also didn't want to risk them insisting I stay behind in case I became unnecessarily aggressive during her rescue, but now I'm seeing why it could have been an issue. Keeping my Drake under control is turning out to be a lot harder than I was prepared for.

"What's going on with you?" Derryn asks me softly, the two of us following close behind while keeping our eyes open for any movement.

I give him the side eye and grunt, not wanting to get into it, and thankfully Derryn gets the drift and doesn't question me any further. Instead, he picks up the pace and overtakes the others, taking position in front, for extra protection.

The rest of the walk passes in absolute silence except for the shuffling of Havana's rapid steps, her short little legs working overtime to keep up with our much longer strides. My awe for her skyrockets when she never slows down or complains in any way; the pure need for survival taking over and powering her through at a speed someone that small should have serious trouble maintaining.

The feline shifters flank both sides of us as we start climbing back up the hill and out of view from the village behind us, with

Neville hot on our heels. It isn't until we reach our original hiding place and sit down to rest for a moment that Scooby flies down to join us, letting us know that Havana's departure went off without a hitch, and no one seemed to notice at all.

With a heavy sigh of relief, Havana's petite body seems to fold in over itself, and she pulls her legs into a tight ball, her head bowed and hidden. It takes me a moment to realise that her shoulders are shaking slightly due to her silent sobs.

Unable to help myself, I sidle up next to her and in my deep tone tell her, "It's going to be okay, little one. You're safe now. I won't let anything happen to you again." Reaching out to touch her slender shoulder, she flinches back and jerks up with wide eyes as if I'd hit her, and I instantly pull my hand back with an apology. "I'm so sorry; I didn't think. I won't hurt you."

But it was too late, the damage was already done. With one thoughtless movement, she seemed to disappear all together, Havana's eyes glazing over and her body going limp like a rag doll. I grab her before she topples over and stare down at her in shock, not sure what the fuck just happened.

"Dude, what did you do?" Neville asks.

I shrug and look between the surprised faces of the males around me. "I have no idea. She just flopped down." I shake her slightly and call out her name, but she just stares off into the distance, like she's empty inside.

"I think we'd better leave," Sebastian recommends, standing up and taking in our position. "The sooner we get out of here, the safer she'll be."

Always the cautious one, I know Sebastian's right. Getting up, I gather her in my arms like a small child and start taking off without hesitation. I say a sharp, "Let's go," as I stalk away.

I know I should be more polite, but Sebastian's reminder that

Havana's still in danger is enough to make my gut twist and light a fire under my overgrown ass.

"Should we shift?" Baxter asks. "It'll be a lot quicker, and Neville could hold her on your back safely during the trip."

A guttural growl rips from me, and I bare my teeth at Neville. The very idea of his arms wrapped around my Kindred is enough to make me want to rip his head off and eat his entrails.

"Whoa," Neville cries, with his arms up in surrender, taking two big steps back, obvious terror in his wide eyes. "I won't hurt her," he defends, looking between me and the others, confused. The scent of his fear permeates the air, and I internally cringe; the last thing I want is to scare my alley and friend. With a deep inhale, I convince my inner beast to calm down and remind him that it's the best way to get her to safety as soon as possible.

I nod stiffly and step toward Neville; he flinches at my approach, and I quickly state, "I'm sorry, my beast overreacted. The sight of this small female in such a fragile state has him in knots." My excuse isn't good enough, and I know that, but it's going to have to do for now, and it must suffice because Neville and the others relax a little. Lifting Havana towards Neville, I reluctantly say, "Take her, and be careful with her."

Before the others can question me about my unusual behaviour, I tear off my clothes and let my Drake out. I've always been known as the calm one, grounding and patient. My inner element is the earth and because of that, my species has always had a centre of calm that most other shifters don't possess. But finding my Kindred, and in such a disturbing way, has my Drake on edge and volatile for the first time in over a century. The last time I was feeling this feral was during our last faction war. The women and innocent bystanders, slain, ripped my insides apart. I still remember their soft bodies torn and broken; I always will.

I huff and lower myself for Neville to climb upon my back safely. With my head turned to watch the males at my side, I pay close attention to Havana being passed tentatively to Sebastian's waiting arms as Neville climbs up. Reaching down, he pulls the small female into his thick arms, his long dirty blond hair falling over his face.

"I've got her," Neville states, shifting her body in front of him carefully. "Pass me the bag with your clothes in it when you're ready, and then we'll be good to go."

He better not drop her. A low rumble sounds from my chest, and the males around me pause again and turn to meet my slitted eyes. I turn my head to the front and huff again, not wanting to deal with their curious gazes.

With everyone shifted, except Matthew, he comes around to my large head and looks up at me, asking quietly, "Are you alright? You seem out of sorts." I blink purposefully and give a small nod in response. "Alright, but you and I will have a chat when we get back to your place. Something tells me you need a stiff drink and an ear." Stripping down, he adds his stuff into the bag and passes it to Neville before shifting into his large white Owl and taking off in front of us.

Grateful that he didn't push it yet, I pull myself up carefully and race behind him, my focus on the bodies on my back. I pay close attention to how secure they feel while I run at such a fast speed. Happy that they aren't jostling too much, I turn my focus to getting back to my home as quickly as my large legs will take me. The others can catch up. They know where I'm going.

* * *

LEON

"Where the fuck is she?" I shout, fury oozing out of every pore, barely containing my beast.

My pathetic excuse for a mother tentatively enters the tower room behind me, and I turn to her with a snarl. "Where is she, wretch?"

She visibly pales and shrinks before my rage, as she should. With a pitiful whimper, she whispers, "I don't know, sir." But I see her eyes shift away with the lie.

I step heavily over to her and grip her fragile, wrinkled neck in my unyielding grasp. "Liar," I growl. "I'll ask you one more time, and if you don't tell me right now, I'll rip your useless life from this world."

With a defiance I've never seen before twinkling in her greying eyes, she tilts her head up and clasps her lips tightly together. *You little bitch.* I grab her thinning white hair with my other hand and pull her behind me without a word. She trips over herself and falls down as I start to descend the stairs. Without looking back at her, I drag her disgusting form all the way down, a heavy thud with each step, strands of her hair ripping out of her scalp as we go.

My body trembles with more and more fury with each passing second. My child has been taken from me. That fucking rodent had the nerve to take my heir from me, and I *will* make her pay. When I catch her, she'll wish she was never born. I'll put her in the dungeon where she belongs and breed her until she dies.

Snarls rip out of me when I enter the centre of my village, the males around us staring with wide eyes as I lead Verna behind me by her hair. I throw her ahead of me, and she slumps down into a ball, her hands clasping her torn and bleeding scalp.

"My breeder is gone!" I yell out, catching the gaze of the males now surrounding us. I point down at her. "This fiend had something to do with it. Who of you knows anything about how my breeder got out?"

I watch as they look between each other with shock and confusion, and it's obvious that nobody before me saw anything out of the ordinary.

"Sir. Sir." I turn to see one of my guards running over, face red and eyes wide. "Two of the guards are dead and beheaded at the rear door."

Someone has trespassed on my territory and stolen my property underneath my nose. *They've taken my child!*

I look at Verna, and she sits back up, her spine straight and proud for the first time ever. Her lips turn up with a defiant smile at my ire, and it's the last straw, tipping my last remnants of control over.

My clothes tear from my violently shaking body as rage consumes me, and the Leviathan within rips to the fore. My beast takes control, and I grow exponentially in size. The blue and green scales ripple over my new form, and my slitted eyes take in the trembling crowd below me.

Verna catches my eye as she scrambles backwards on her hands and feet like a scared little crab. With a monstrous roar that shakes the very foundation of my village, I let loose my fury into the sky. My large clawed foot slams down on Verna's retreating body, forcing a scream from her as her lower body crushes from my heavy weight. Leaning down, I snap my mouth over her and rip the top half of her body apart from the rest and gulp it down the back of my throat. Lifting the rest of the bloody mess of what was once my mother with my front claw, I throw her lower torso and legs into my mouth and swallow her remains whole.

Still in a rage, I take my hatred of my breeder out on the males around me; I stomp those stupid enough to still be around me. Roaring all the while, and unable to tamp down my normally pristine control.

CHAPTER NINE

HAVANA

A terrifying roar carries over the valley we just passed, stirring me awake and shaking me to the core. The guy behind me tightens his hold around my waist, and I cringe inwardly at his touch.

"Are you alright?" he asks me delicately, as though I might break at any moment, and he might not be wrong. My sanity feels temporary at this stage, my mental capacity pushed to its limit.

Choosing to ignore him, I look sideways and down at the beast that we're riding, a frown deepening on my face. *What the heck is this thing*? Seeming to understand my wary look, the man behind me explains, "That's Hermes. He's the only one big enough to comfortably carry us, and it's a lot quicker than walking."

I lie down to go back to sleep, and my hands flatten on the Dragon thing below me; the earthy brown hue of his scales, both hard and soft to the touch. Each one is immovable under my hands like armour but the texture against my fingertips as I gently stroke them feels smooth, almost like a moss or velvet. It fascinates me because it's nothing like I expected.

Finding out that the giant Viking man was the monster below me wasn't at all surprising. There was no way he was something sweet, like a dolphin or flamingo. I almost smile at that thought because it would be hilarious seeing him turn into the fluffy pink bird.

Closing my eyes, I let my exhaustion float me away on the wings of sleep. Reality comes and goes for me over the next couple of days, and I don't always know what's real and what's a dream.

At one point, I overhear the men talking quietly about me and eavesdrop, keeping my eyes closed and my breathing even so they think I'm asleep. They act differently when they think I'm asleep, and I'm still trying to decide if I can trust them or not. So far, nobody has touched me inappropriately or done anything that would show me they don't mean me any harm, but I've learned not to trust too easily, and I'm not about to start now.

"We'll stay with you at your place until she needs to be moved to a different location, or she finds her Kindred," one of the men says, his voice has a musical lilt to it, and it reminds me of the man who was sitting behind me on the monster.

"Aye. I'll nae be leaving for sure," the Scottish man replies. "She'll need all the protection she can get because there's nae a chance that Leon will just let us take her without a fight."

Leon's name makes me shudder in disgust, and I quickly push back the memories of him touching me before I disappear into myself again. Wanting to hear more of what they're saying, I try to focus on them instead.

"I appreciate any assistance in keeping the female safe. Thank you," the deep husky voice of Hermes says, the rumble of it rolls along my skin like a caress. For some reason, he affects me more than the others, not necessarily in a bad way, but it's a new feeling that I can't quite put my finger on, and it makes me uneasy.

"It's a shame that none of us have her as a Kindred," another voice that I can't place adds sullenly. "At least then she would have that as an extra protection."

A scoff sounds off. "No way. It would just be an unwelcome hassle with a mission like this. I mean, she's pretty and all that, but with the way she's been mistreated by Leon, the male would be unable to focus on what we have to do and instead be either hell-bent on mating with her or getting revenge on the Leviathan. It would be a catastrophe."

Sounds of agreement come from the surrounding men. The burden it would be to have me as their Kindred obvious, and their relief at not being mine, a sharp pain in my chest. *Will nobody be able to love me? Even here?*

"What if *Leon* is her Kindred?" another guy asks.

Immediately, Hermes' baritone voice snaps, "He's not. If he was, he never would have treated her that way. Plus, we would smell it on her."

"I don't know," someone replies. "You know what that faction is like. I'll tell you one thing though, he better not be, because if he is, he'll never stop trying to get her back. At this point, I'm just hoping that he doesn't care too much and will just go back to the market."

"How is that better?" the Scottish man asks. "It'll just mean a different lass needs saving."

They continue to talk amongst themselves for a while, more about their packs and families, and I eventually drift back off to sleep thinking about the baby growing in my stomach and praying to God that Leon doesn't come after me for it, but knowing deep down that he'll never stop until he takes it from me.

I vow with my last conscious thought that I'll do whatever it takes to keep this baby safe, and if that means giving it to a stronger person to protect, then I'll do it in a heartbeat.

I've got you, my little bean. Mummy will protect you.

* * *

HERMES

The trip back to my territory seems so much longer than it would normally be, even though we're technically making good time. I'm driven by a primal need to get Havana into my safe haven, the need to cook for her, protect her, make her smile, and touch her without her flinching.

We have to stop for two nights along the way, and Havana goes in and out of her strange state of consciousness. Every time she comes to, I make an effort to talk to her and feed her, but she just locks back down again, and I'm yet to hear her utter a single sound.

As my frustration and confusion grows within me at each silent moment from her, Derryn pulls me aside at our last stop before home to talk to me privately. "I'll be honest with you, Hermes. You're making us all nervous. Between your grumpy mood and your Drake randomly growling at everybody, it's a wee bit concerning. Should we be worried that you're going to flip on us?"

"Shit," I mumble. "No. Of course not. I don't know what's wrong with me. I'm feeling extremely protective of Havana. She's just so small, and she never says or does anything; it's freaking me out and putting me on edge," I explain, rubbing my beard nervously.

Derryn pats me on the shoulder in a friendly way. We've been close for many years now; I've known him and his twin Baine since they were just tykes. Their da too. That's one of the bonuses of living for such a long time. I get to watch families grow and change over the centuries. The negative side, however, means that I also get a front-row seat to the losses of so many loved ones. Females don't fare well in our world or live anywhere as long as they should, as much as I wish that it wasn't so.

Derryn and Baine's Da is only alive today because their mother wasn't his Kindred; he was just lucky enough that they fell in love with each other, but just like most females in Rathe, she met an untimely demise when the boys were only two years old. He was never the same again and took a posting on Earth with them at the embassy in Scotland, determined to keep them safe. When they reached thirteen, the Celestials sent word via the Angels that they were to return to Rathe where they belonged, and I happily took them both under my wing until they found packs of their own.

It brings me great pride and joy knowing that Baine now lives with his Kindred and has twins of his own. Regardless of them not being wolves, they are very much his. Apparently, Havana is a good friend of his Kindred's too, which is very exciting. I can only hope that Derryn will have the same fortunate outcome from this wave of females.

"I nae want to tell you how to deal with this, but you ken that Janice said Havana dinnae speak to males," Derryn reminds me softly. "Maybe she'll nae get better when we get to your house. You need to be prepared for that. I see how upset it makes you when she dinnae reply to you. Plus, you're a huge fecking guy, and she's got to be scared to death at how scary you look. Nae offence."

I let out a small chuckle because he's not wrong. Compared to the others, I'm a tad intimidating, not that the other males here aren't either, but my size and tattoos cement how people view me. Being a giant Drake certainly doesn't help.

"I know. I know," I acknowledge. "Thanks for reminding me.

I'll make more of an effort to tone my shit down, and I might give her a wider birth until we reach home. Perhaps when she has her own room, Havana might relax a bit more and stop disappearing inside herself. I hate it when she does that. I feel so helpless, and that's a new feeling for me."

"Right," Derryn smacks his hands together and says loud enough for everyone to hear him. "Let's get going. It's getting late, and we're almost there. The wee lass has fallen asleep again; let's nae wake her."

With a collective affirmative, we set out on the last trek of our long journey, careful not to rouse Havana. The first tendrils of relief fill me, knowing how close we are to my territory.

I hope she likes her new home. I hope she'll accept it as her home. I hope she'll accept me...

CHAPTER TEN

HAVANA

Feeling rested and comfortable, I roll over and stretch my body with a deep yawn. No nightmares follow me from the depths, and I let a small smile slip before I realise I'm in a bed, and I shouldn't be.

My eyes snap open in shock, and I bolt upright. *Where the heck am I?*

Looking down at my body, I sigh in relief to see myself still fully clothed, and I slowly take in my surroundings. The bed I'm in is big enough for three people, with dark wood and wrought iron bed ends, and a thick, dark-green blanket covers me. The room is surprisingly large with matching furniture, two green settees in front of an open fireplace, three wooden doors, and what looks like a sizable glass sliding door covered with curtains in the same dark-green hue.

From what I understood from the men when I was

eavesdropping, this must be Hermes' house. He's obviously a fan of green, going by the room decor.

I listen carefully but can't hear anything other than my own breathing. Deciding to check out what's on the other side of the doors around the room, I gingerly get out of the comfortable bed and stalk to the heavy curtains. Pulling them aside, I'm shocked to only see my reflection because of the pitch-black night outside. It's so dark that I can't make out anything. Not wanting to open the door to an unknown area late at night, I close the curtains and move over to the first wooden door. A walk in robe greets me, and I surprisingly notice that the dark room has some women's clothing hung on a few coat hangers, not many but enough for me to wonder whose clothes they are.

Closing the door again, I move over to the door beside it and gasp in surprise at the lavish bathroom before me. I switch on the light beside me that instantly illuminates the soft cream room. A toilet sits on the left, a sink on the right, and at the back is a huge bath sunken in the floor, big enough for at least four people, and an open shower that has a wide shower head on the roof above. The dark green towels and bath mat aren't a surprise to me, but it brings a smile to my lips, knowing that so much thought was put into this place.

A knock comes from the remaining door, and I suck in a nervous breath, slowly walking to it. Grasping the brass handle, I exhale and open it only an inch, to find the Owl shifter Matthew smiling down at me.

"Hey there, sunshine," he greets cheerfully. "I was going past and heard you walking around and thought I'd better let you know where you are and that you're safe."

I open it fully and smile timidly at him but keep a good distance between us, my hand still clasped onto the door handle in case I need to shut it.

Realising that he's not getting anything further out of me, he asks, "Are you hungry?" He steps back and puts his hands behind his back, an obvious sign that he's no threat to me, and I relax my shoulders slightly. "Hermes just finished making dinner, and there's a full plate of hot food downstairs with your name on it."

Matthew's friendly features have me relaxing even more, and before I get to decline, my stomach groans emphatically at the mention of food. I'm actually starving, and the smell of something delicious floats down the hall, tempting me to leave my safe little haven.

"Well now," Matthew starts with a chuckle, "I'm pretty sure you can't say no after that declaration."

My face heats, and I feel my cheeks redden in embarrassment. I lick my dry lips, nervous about stepping out of the room but unable to deny my hunger, I step forward with a small nod.

Looking down at the floor, I close the door behind me and wait for Matthew to show me the way. Picking up my cue, he turns and stalks down the brightly lit hallway and down a flight of wide stairs. The dark wood balustrade is decorated with intricate wrought iron patterns of leaves and vines, and I can't help but run my fingers along them as I descend the staircase.

I hear someone suck in their breath sharply and look up to find Hermes at the bottom, staring up at me with a look I can't decipher. Perhaps longing? But that can't be right.

Dropping my eyes once more, I continue to follow Matthew to the dining room just off to the left. He pulls out a seat for me at the end of the long table, away from the men clustered around the other end, and tells me to sit, moving down to his own seat with the others.

Grateful that I don't have to sit near any of the men, I sit down quietly, pulling my chair in beneath me, surprised by the heavy weight of it. Is everything here heavy wood? I suppose I should be used to that by now. Wood is definitely a household staple in Rathe.

I give a quick look up in the guys' direction, and I happily notice they're making a point not to look at me, realising how uncomfortable I am in their presence. The other head of the table is empty, the chair pulled out but with no one in it. It's then that I see that Hermes is missing from the room.

Speaking of the devil, his considerable frame walks through the open space holding two loaded plates; his gaze drifting over to me immediately. With a few large strides, his body slides into my space and I tense, staring down at my hands in my lap. The heat from his body warms my side, and I gulp hard at his nearness.

Ever so carefully, Hermes places the first plate in front of me, and I notice that the room has gone silent, everyone seemingly holding their breath, waiting for my response. I nod slowly in thanks, unable to utter a word, my mouth dry and my heart racing in panic because he's close to me, too close.

"You're welcome," he states simply, and not in a sarcastic way, but a gracious one. Moving away, he continues to give everybody a plate of dinner, and it's only then that I take note of the meal before me.

A huge serving of what seems to be roast beef fills my plate, with an array of juicy looking vegetables. I haven't had a meal like this in so long that I can't even remember what it was. The heavenly smell of meat and gravy fills my mouth with saliva once more, and I raise my shaking hand to the fork beside it, unable to wait a second more to taste it.

Picking up a piece of thick beef, I stuff it in my mouth in a very unladylike manner and a low moan seeps out of me, my eyes sliding closed in pure ecstasy.

Clank.

A loud noise makes me jump, and my eyes pop open to see all

the men staring at me with wide eyes and open jaws. Hermes' fork had dropped onto the plate before him, his breathing heavy and his focus squarely on my mouth.

Feeling embarrassed at my accidental moan, I raise both hands to my mouth and drop my gaze again, my eyes burning with unshed tears because of the weighty attention on me. I want to shrink, to disappear. I want to leave.

Just as my feet go to jump up and run me from this place, Matthew groans over dramatically with a, "This is fucking epic, Drake. Where have you been all my life?"

The other men around the table start laughing and sharing in the enthusiasm over such a yummy meal, and I'm overwhelmingly thankful for Matthew's ridiculous performance. I return my focus to my meal and am mindful not to make another sound, while listening to the easy, happy banter at the other end of the table. It's clear that they're going out of their way to make me feel comfortable and not pressuring me to get involved with being social.

I, unbelievably, finished the entire plate of roast because it was so freaking good that I didn't want to miss out on even one bite. Unfortunately, because I have been eating hardly anything for so long, it doesn't take long for my stomach to revolt at the amount of food I shoved into it.

Nausea starts to take over, and I slowly rise from the table, hoping to God that I don't vomit it all back onto my plate, but by the time I'm fully standing I know that my time is limited, and I turn and run from the room, bolting up the stairs as fast as I can and throwing myself into my bedroom, barely making it to my toilet on time.

With violent heaving, I lose my delicious dinner again, and I sob in between each retch, devastated that I didn't get to keep it. I make a mental note as the tears slide down my face to only eat half of my next meal, no matter how good it tastes.

"Oh, little one," Hermes' deep voice murmurs behind me, lifting my crazy mane of hair away from my face, tenderly tying it up in a messy bun for me.

Unable to move from the toilet bowl, I have no choice but to let him take care of me. Thankfully, he doesn't touch me beyond doing up my hair.

When I'm all vomited out, I sit back on my heels and rest my cheek on the toilet seat. I watch in disbelief as Hermes grabs a glass beside the bathroom sink, filling it with water before sitting surprisingly gracefully beside me on the floor. "Here you go. Drink it slowly," he says softly as he passes me the glass.

I take an apprehensive sip of the cool liquid and am glad for the soothing feel of it down my sore throat. Closing my eyes, I lean my head back down.

"Do you think you're done?" Hermes asks me, and I nod with my eyes still closed, exhaustion filling me once more. I don't think I'll ever feel normal again, not that I ever did, I suppose.

Hearing Hermes standing back up, I open my eyes and find his hand before me. "Come now, little one, it's time for you to get back into bed." I look at his hand nervously but take it, knowing that I need the help to get up. My body feels heavy, the toll of the past few days weighing me down and insisting I rest.

Hermes gently helps me to my feet and guides me back out to my bed, lifting the sheets open for me. "Do you want to get changed first?" he asks, but I shake my head, only wanting to sleep for now. "Okay, hop on in, and I'll leave the bedside lamp on for you and turn off the other lights when I leave. How does that sound?"

I tuck myself into bed and nod, my eyes closing the second my head dropped onto the fluffy pillow. *It's been so long since I was comfortable.* Hermes' heavy footfalls move away from me, and he turns out the light, closing the door softly behind him.

My mind wanders, filling my head with thoughts of the baby inside me. *Was I sick because of the pregnancy, or was it just too much food? Does baby bean not like beef? Are you okay in there, Baby Bean? What am I going to do with you? Should I tell the men about you? No, I don't think so. Let's get through this together for now, Bean. Just you and me.*

I think about what I need to do in order to take care of it. Maybe Summer's pack will let me come home to them? I miss her, and she's always been so nice to me, but is it selfish to bring my problems to her when she has her own babies to worry about, not to mention her other four kids? How does she do it? I'm scared about having just this one.

At least I have some time before I have to figure out what to do. Bean and I will figure it out eventually, because we have to.

CHAPTER ELEVEN

HERMES

"All I'm saying is that it's been almost two weeks, and there's been absolutely no sign of retaliation," Neville states with his arms wide. "I was expecting some kind of fight back, but nobody followed us, and there's been zero evidence of anyone following us here. They might have no clue where she was taken."

Playing with a stray braid, I listen to his reasoning, and he's not wrong. The rescue went off without a hitch. "I get what you're saying and if you feel like the threat to her is passing, then by all means, feel free to go home. I would ask if any of you would agree to stay, even if it's just until Blayze comes, to make sure that there's some backup if something goes wrong," I say. Not because I don't think I can keep her safe, but because the safer I can make Havana, the better.

"I'll be staying on as long as you need me," Matthew answers easily, leaning back with his feet on my table. I whack them off, and he laughs, always the jokester. "It's not like I have anywhere pressing to be. I've got no family or pack."

Scooby agrees wholeheartedly. "Same goes for me. We'll be good lookouts during the night, anyway. If there's going to be any kind of attack, it'll probably be then, and I'm happy to help out."

"Are you sure you don't mind if I head back?" Baxter asks warily. "I'll stay if you think it necessary. I'm just not used to being away from the coalition for long periods of time. We tend to stay close to home. Plus, I heard we're getting new females sent to us soon, and I'd hate to miss out."

Baxter has always been a reliable Cheetah and a great warrior, but his beast tends to get homesick after a while, and I'd hate to cause him any unnecessary discomfort.

"Like I said, friend, it's totally fine with me. Having Scooby and Matthew here will be enough to put my mind at ease, especially since I'll be able to sleep in peace knowing that you guys are out there," I state, honestly.

"I'll take my leave too, then, Hermes," Sebastian adds. "But I'm not far from here, as you know, so just give off a loud roar, and I'll be here in no time at all. My Panther is fast, and I won't let you down."

Derryn gets up with a stretch, looking over the vast horizon from the balcony we're sitting on. "I hope you ken I'm nae so easy to get rid of? Plus, if I went anywhere while Havana is possibly at risk, Baine would have my balls for leaving his lass's friend. I ken he'd do the same for me. Nae to mention, I'm determined to get Havana to laugh before I take my leave."

"I think you've hung around Keneth too much at Threshold," I say with a laugh, remembering Summer's pet name for him. "You've confused yourself with being funny."

Derryn flips me the bird and walks off muttering, "Feck off. I can be funny."

We all laugh at his departure, and I look out at the view, thinking of the beautiful girl hidden away in her room. *I wonder what she'll think of it?*

The wind blows chilly air around us, and I scowl as I imagine how Havana is going to deal with the cold climate here. The sun shines down warmly, but the climate here can get on the freezing side because my home is built into the mountainside, the snowy mountains just beyond this one. *Do I even have any warm clothes for her?* Drakes don't feel the cold much, so it's never been an issue for me before now.

"How do I talk to the female about what she needs if she doesn't ever talk to me?" I ask the males around me. "She barely even looks at me, so how do I know what she wants?"

Baxter laughs out loud. "That's a conundrum for the ages, my friend. Even if she didn't stop talking, I can guarantee that you still wouldn't know what she wants. The females don't even know."

"I've heard that too, actually," Matthew says, pulling on his bottom lip in thought. "How do they manage that?"

"Who knows? They're the magical creatures, if you ask me," Baxter replies.

While I'm happy for the playful banter, I am deeply worried about how I'm supposed to fulfill all of her needs when I can't just ask her. Havana is by far the most challenging woman that I've come across in my long years, but I don't mind that one bit. I just wish I knew how to make her happy. Witnessing her vomit all of her food up the other night broke my heart because she clearly savoured every bite, but I made a note to give her half of the serving I'd normally feed someone else from now on. I don't want to be responsible for making her sick; she needs every bit of nourishment that she can get.

* * *

HAVANA

Not sure if I have the right to roam freely through the house, or if I'm meant to stay in my given quarters, I've spent all my time, other than meals, in my room looking longingly at the world beyond my window.

I've never been an outdoorsy person, but after being confined in Leon's tower for so long, I feel trapped and claustrophobic here. The long plains and rocky hills beyond call to me. I think I'd honestly be happy to just roam the vast house on the other side of my bedroom door.

Feeling uncharacteristically bold, I clasp the door handle with a deep exhale and quietly pull it open, peeking my head through the gap and glancing down the well-lit hallway.

Merry sounds of men laughing and talking boisterously float throughout the house, and I try to remember that nobody here wants to hurt me and that they've been nothing but hospitable to me. It's easier said than done, though. The years of abuse I've dealt with since such a young age has gripped me by the throat and refuses to let go; to let me breathe and relax.

Memories of Summer and Janice laughing and playing with the men back with my old pack fill me, while I sat quietly on the sidelines, taking it all in and wishing that I knew how to be so carefree and brave. All my life I've been on the outside looking in, the visceral fear of everything around me, crippling. Even if I was free to roam all of Rathe, I wouldn't, couldn't. My most constricting cage by far is myself.

Gathering all of my courage, I step through the door and tiptoe down the hall to the top of the stairs; my bare feet not making a sound. Earlier I put on a flowy, chocolate-brown dress I found in the back of my closet but didn't find any shoes to fit my petite feet. Although, I'm totally okay with that because I've never really liked shoes and tend to wear them as little as possible, only putting on my jandals if absolutely necessary.

The size of this grand home always takes me by surprise. It is a home and not just a house though, because Hermes has made it into one. Everyone here seems comfortable and at ease, especially with him being such an accommodating host, always with a scrumptious meal, a smile, or a glass to toast with. I find it hard to come to terms with the scary image of Hermes and his gentle, patient manner. He's an oxymoron if I've ever seen one.

With slow, stealthy movements, I make my way down the stairs and follow the sound of merriment, stopping at the edge of a large open balcony where most of the men seem to be hanging out. I keep my body hidden around the side of the heavy drapery and look over the mix of men outside; the only thing similar about them is their beauty. Beauty probably isn't the right word for what they are, though, but I don't know any word that will suffice for the men in Rathe. Perfect, perhaps?

"Motley crew of lads, aren't they?" Derryn asks behind me, and I jump in shock, an involuntary squeak escaping. "Surely you're like a little field mouse, tiptoeing around the house and squeaking."

I raise my hand to my thumping heart, my eyes wide as I try to calm my breathing.

"Come on, wee mouse, come outside and old Derryn'll hook you up with a drink," he says with a smile, his arm out towards the balcony.

It doesn't pass my notice that the men outside are now silent. Obviously, my squeak got everybody's attention, and I feel my cheeks heat in embarrassment as I stare at the floor and join them.

A chair screeches back and Hermes' deep voice says, "Please, take my seat." He stands and offers me his place at the table, stepping back away from it as if I'll bite him, but I know he's just trying to give me some space, and I appreciate it.

Sitting down gingerly, I nod in thanks, my eyes lifting no higher than his broad chest. His size is still shocking to me, especially when he's in my vicinity. It really reveals the size difference between us.

A chilly wind flows through the breeze-way and my body shivers, my arms wrapping around myself trying to keep warm.

Hermes steps forward, clenching and unclenching his fists like he wants to grab for something, and my body tenses up again. Noticing my discomfort, he steps back again and shakes his head, his long braids falling over his shoulders.

"Are you cold, female?" Hermes asks, while the other men sit quietly, studying us both. Before I get a chance to reply, he strides back into the house like his ass is on fire.

"Alrighty," Baxter starts, "I guess he's on a mission. Havana, a couple of the other males and I have to get back home, but Derryn, Matthew, and Scooby will be here with you and Hermes as extra protection. If you really need him, Sebastian's not too far from here."

My head pops up, a mix of emotions rolling through me. Relief because that must mean that Leon won't come after me here. Fear of what happens if he does. And something else that I can't put my finger on. The idea of almost being alone with Hermes makes me nervous somehow.

Hermes reappears at my side, holding a large fur blanket, his arms stretched out to me in offer. "Here, little one, use this. I'm sorry that I forgot how fragile humans are to the cold."

Way to make me feel smaller than I already do. The way Hermes acts around me makes it seem like I might shatter into a million shards of glass if he's not careful; I suppose he's not entirely wrong.

I take it from him and wrap it around my back, crossing it over in the front, feeling an instant relief from the cold air.

"It's okay, mouse, we don't need these Muppets, anyway. Thunder and lightning will keep you safe," Derryn says with a laugh, kissing his biceps. Unable to help myself, a small smile lifts the corner of my mouth.

Hermes growls deeply. His eyes narrowed on the Scot, my smile dropping immediately at the terrifying sound.

"I can protect her," he booms, leaning over the table, his eyes turning dark.

Derryn's eyebrows raise, and Matthew puts his hands up, garnering both of their attention. "Hey, hey, hey. No one's saying you can't, brother. It was just a joke to lighten the mood," Matthew says calmly. "How about we get some lunch started? I don't know about you guys, but I'm starving. Feel like some help in the kitchen today, Hermes?"

The tension in the air drops, and Hermes nods tightly, turning to me. "Do you like burgers?" he asks softly. His mood swings are confusing.

I nod in affirmation and try but fail to smile.

"Great. It's settled then, burgers for lunch. I hope you like pickles because I have a tendency to add too many, I've been told," he adds, rubbing his hands together with a smile. His love for food is actually quite contagious, and his meals never fail to make me feel better.

The thought of pickles has me swallowing deeply. I've never minded them, but right now I'm salivating at the idea. I nod more enthusiastically this time, meeting his pleased eyes briefly.

Matthew stands and pats Scooby on the back. "Sucks to be you, mate." He laughs and says to Hermes as they head towards the kitchen, "The fucker hates pickles."

CHAPTER TWELVE

HAVANA

A month has passed without a single sign from Leon, and I find myself relaxing into my new normal more and more every day.

Derryn and Matthew have taken it upon themselves to try to make me laugh or smile as often as they can, which to their dismay isn't that often at all. As much as I want to fully relax, I just can't. There's too much up in the air.

What if they find out that I'm pregnant and send me back to Leon because it's his baby I'm carrying? I don't fully know how it works here, but I don't want to take the chance because in this place I have space, security, and nobody wants anything from me or takes anything without asking. I haven't been in a daze for weeks now.

Hermes seems to have retreated into himself more than when I first got here, and I think it's somehow my fault. I find him staring at me all the time with a look of longing, and it seems like he's waiting for me to say or do something, but I don't know what.

I still haven't spoken to anyone, and I don't really feel the need to. Words aren't necessary for me; they're just fillers that make me anxious and uncomfortable. I don't mind listening to the guys chat and quite often find myself just hanging out in their vicinity doing my own thing like cross stitch. A passion I've found since coming here, Scooby got me into it, and now I don't seem to be able to stop, despite the fact that I can't see for shit. There's been a couple of minor nips of the needle on my fingers, but I've figured out how to work around it by touch.

I'm usually either sitting in front of the fireplace, lounging in my bedroom, or wrapped up in my favourite fur blanket on the balcony; the one that Hermes gave me that feels like ages ago.

Unfortunately, I have become quite ill with morning sickness lately and hiding it has been super hard. When the guys figure out that I've been throwing up, they've just narrowed it down to me eating too much again. Also, morning sickness is a total lie. I feel sick constantly and get very little warning before I lose my last meal. It could be as simple as a small smell setting me off.

It's a real shame when I do lose my dinner because Hermes' cooking is the best I've ever had. He is a master in the kitchen, whether it's a fancy five-star meal or macaroni and cheese. He nails it every time.

Pickles and tomato juice have become my go-to snacks. Apparently, this baby has really odd taste buds, and I'm not even mad because it's so freaking yum.

* * *

HERMES

I can't stay away from her, but I can't approach her either. Having my Kindred share my home with me is both a dream and a nightmare because she can't stand the sight of me.

Every time I manage to get anywhere near Havana, the rancid scent of her fear makes me want to vomit. It seems that it's just me that makes her react that way.

I watch in morbid fascination as she smiles at Matthew by the fireplace; her small elegant fingers working overtime on the floral cross stitch she's working on, while Matthew tells her funny stories about his little brother not being able to figure out how to fly when he first started shifting. The story lights up her beautiful brown eyes with humour, obviously enjoying how funny it is.

What I wouldn't give to be the reason that she smiled, to be the person her eyes lit up for. But I would happily sit quietly by and let someone else do it, if it means she knows some measure of happiness.

"Brother, come and join us," Matthew tells me cheerfully. "There's enough room for us all by the hearth."

He has always been a good friend to me, and the last month has been no different. While I try not to wallow in self-pity, snapping and growling at Matthew and the others over the stupidest things, he has been nothing but patient and understanding with me, making me feel a million times worse than I already did. I've been such a bad friend lately, but I can't seem to be able to reel my beast in when it comes to the other males being around my Kindred.

I stalk forward, purposely wearing a soft smile, and sit on the chair beside Havana. Her shoulders tense, and her hands freeze on the spot.

The scent of her fear travels to me instantly, and my spine

stiffens as my beast fights for dominance; the need to protect her driving me hard, but it's me that she's scared of, and I don't know what to do about that. I always keep my voice low. I give her lots of space, and I give her anything she could possibly need, but Havana goes on fearing me, regardless.

Resigned to my fate, I sigh heavily and stand back up. "I'll go. Sorry for intruding."

As I start walking away, my head low in defeat, two almost silent words have me stopping in my tracks and my head whirling around to face my Kindred. "I'm sorry."

Her sweet voice is huskier and lower than I expected. The gentle melody of those simple words wash over me, and I shudder at the warmth billowing from my heart. *She spoke. To me.*

Matthew sucks in a sharp breath, and my eyes lock with Havana's, our gazes unable to stray.

"Never apologise to me, little one, your happiness is the most important thing to me, and I understand how I must look to you," I say honestly, because I'll deal with whatever she needs to go through to keep her happy.

Her eyes drop back down to her work, and she nods slightly, her little hand trembling as she tries to thread the needle.

I turn to Matthew and find his eyes wide and staring at me like he's just had an epiphany. A wide grin forms on his face as he looks between Havana and me, and I know in that instant that he just figured out my little secret.

He opens his mouth to say something, but I shake my head quickly, nodding in her direction. Getting the hint, Matthew stands up slowly and says to Havana, "I'm gonna go have a beer with Hermes. Are you alright here for a bit?"

She shoos him away, and he laughs at being dismissed. "I guess only you get words from the female," he jokes loud enough for her to hear as we leave the room together.

As soon as we are out of view and hearing range, Matthew grabs me by the shoulder, spinning me around with a, "What the fuck, dude?"

I shrug like I don't know what he's talking about, and he gives me the stink eye.

"She's your Kindred," Matthew exclaims in a loud whisper, and it's not a question. I just cross my arms over my chest and stare him down. "Are you really just gonna stand there and not say anything? Why didn't you tell us?"

Matthew's shock starts to turn into anger as I continue to ignore his accusation.

"Fuck that, man, why haven't you told her?" he asks louder and I shush him. "Have you ever thought that it would make her feel better to know that she has a Kindred looking out for her?"

Having enough of his judgement, I growl out, "You're kidding, right? She can't even stand to be in the same room as me. She seems more scared of my shadow than the idea of Leon coming after her. She'd be terrified to hear that I'm what she's stuck with." My voice breaks at the end, and my friend's eyes soften at the truth of my words. "If I thought it would help, I'd tell her, but I honestly think it'll just make things worse for her."

"It's about time you admitted that she's your lass," Derryn says from behind me. "I've been waiting for weeks for someone else to notice."

Matthew's eyes narrow at him as Derryn joins us. "You knew?"

"The real question is, how dinnae you ken when this numpty just sits there pining after her like a sad puppy all day long?" Derryn asks, shaking his head. "I also agree with Hermes. She's nae ready. Havana is only just coming out of her shell, and I ken she needs more time to heal."

I put my hands up in a "See, I told you" gesture and exhale, pissed off that they've figured it out. I'm not ashamed that she's my Kindred, but I am ashamed by how much she dislikes me. I have failed her every day that she fears me, and now everybody will know.

"What about you two?" I ask with a low growl. "Is she yours too?"

I have to bite the inside of my cheek to not lash out at them if they say yes. I know I'm meant to be understanding when there's more than one male Kindred, but my beast is adamant that he won't share and wants to rip off the heads of my friends at the very idea of them even thinking about touching her.

Matthew puts his hands up in surrender at the visceral fury emanating from me. "Calm down. I'm not interested in Havana that way. I look at her more like a little sister, if anything. There's zero attraction there, brother, I swear it."

"Don't bother looking at me," Derryn snorts, unfazed by the lingering threat behind my eyes. "She's a nice lass and all, but there's a female out there with a lovely set of knockers and curves waiting for me, and it ain't her."

Hearing the truth from them both, I visibly relax, my shoulders lumping low. "I'm doing the best I can," I admit, not sure what else to say.

"Be patient. It'll all work out," Matthew says with a smile, his hand squeezing my shoulder in support. "In the meantime, I'll do what I can to talk you up. She'll come around, I'm sure."

I hope so, I really do.

CHAPTER THIRTEEN

HAVANA

I watch with fascination as Derryn's Wolf runs off in the distance, with the other two in their Owl forms flying above. The three of them were hankering for a hunt and because it's super quiet around here, especially since the others left, Hermes told them to go for it and that he'd keep watch for any threats.

The late afternoon sun has lost most of its warmth, and the air is even cooler at this time of day, but the outside calls to me, and before you know it, I've donned a thick fur coat and some way-too-big boots for a mini adventure outside.

Stepping off the bottom step, doubt starts creeping into me about being out here without letting Hermes know where I am. I'd hate to get lost or injured. Deciding not to risk it, I choose to stay close to the house and head left towards Hermes' vegetable patch.

Maybe I'll pick something fresh for dinner. I wonder if he'll let me cook for once?

As I approach the hedges hiding the garden I know it is beyond, I stop at the sound of deep chuckles and hear an unmistakable voice coo, "Hey little fella, you want a carrot?"

The gentle, almost childlike voice Hermes is using has me tilting my head in confusion. *What the heck?* Who's with him?

Another chuckle has me stepping forward quietly and carefully, peeking around the corner to the most shocking sight. I don't know what I was expecting, but it wasn't this.

Hermes is sitting cross-legged in the middle of a vast vegetable garden, backed by various fruit trees and vines filled with delights. All around him is an array of tiny little creatures; bunnies, hedgehogs, squirrels, and field mice, even happy little starlings and hummingbirds flitter around him, landing on plants nearby.

My hand flies to my mouth, desperately trying to hold in a laugh at the thought that the formidable Hermes is Rathe's version of Cinderella. All he needs is a fairy Godmother and one of his pumpkins turning into a chariot.

Unfortunately, my attempts are futile as an uncontrollable giggle flies loose at the mental image, garnering Hermes' attention instantly. His eyes go from shocked to amused in seconds, crinkling in the corners as he smiles widely at me.

"What's so funny, little one?" he chuckles, while patting a particularly snuggly bunny.

I laugh even harder, bending over at the waist and clutching at my stomach. Lost in the humour of Hermes Cinderella, I laugh harder than I think I ever have, my chest heaving for breath and my eyes leaking tears of joy.

Heaving a big sigh, I ask, "Have you ever heard of Cinderella?" I lost it again at his baffled expression.

Hermes starts laughing along with me, shaking his head. "No," he chuckles. "But it must be funny. Breathe, or you'll pass out."

I try to gulp in some big breaths, calming my moment of insanity down, my cheeks aching from laughing and smiling so hard. Sighing with contentment, I rub at my cheeks and look at the cute little animals surprisingly still sitting around Hermes, even after us both laughing loudly.

"Aren't they scared?" I ask incredulously.

Leaning over and giving a bit of fresh lettuce to another bunny, he smiles at them, "Of course not, they know I'd never hurt them," he answers without hesitation.

His answer has me pausing. H*ave I had him all wrong this whole time?* It's hard to look at Hermes now and picture a monster, when he's clearly gentle if these vulnerable, tiny animals trust him so implicitly.

Hermes looks cute, like a giant tattooed child, if anything. His behaviour is so carefree, and his movements seem so thoughtful and tender, as he carefully pats and feeds them.

"You can join me if you'd like?" he says, getting my attention. "Just pick up some veg' on the way and move slowly. They might be wary at first, but they'll come around."

Gliding as slowly as I can, I move towards his own personal petting zoo, picking up some silver beet leaves along the way, holding them in front of me to show them that I'm bringing food.

The birds fly to safe branches nearby and a couple of the animals freeze, with their eyes locked on my every move. All except the white bunny nuzzling into Hermes' leg for more attention. I step close, and they move back enough for me to sit down delicately next to Hermes, who's watching me just as closely as his pets are.

I reach my gathered snack towards his fluffy white bunny, hoping that it will be the one most likely to take food from a stranger. I was right because almost instantly, the little fella twitches his little nose at it and takes a happy little nibble, encouraging his little friend to hop over and join in on my offering of friendship.

My bum wiggles on the ground as I hold in a squeal of delight, not wanting to scare the little fluffies. I look up at Hermes and find his gaze soft and watching me intently, obviously happy with me joining him. His gentle scrutiny has my cheeks pinking with heat.

"How long have you been feeding them? They seem to really like you," I ask, to get his intense focus off me.

He chuckles again and looks down at them with undeniable love. "Seems like forever," Hermes answers. "Before them, I took care of their parents, grandparents, and so on. I've been here for a very long time and this is their home just as much as it is mine, and if I can help to feed and care for them, I will."

His sweet nature has taken me by surprise today, but I'm not really sure why, if I think about it. Since I've been here, he's been nothing but kind and patient with me, giving me anything I ask for and a million things I haven't.

Guilt fills me when I remember all the little things Hermes has done to make me feel at home and safe here, and yet I thanked him by avoiding him like the plague and only spending time with Derryn and Matthew, even Scooby sometimes, but he's pretty reclusive.

When I think about the first time I laid eyes on him, the only thing I saw was how terrifying he was, and not the fact that he was covered in blood for me, going out of his way to risk his own life to take on Leon's guards to rescue me, even though he didn't know me.

I have misjudged this poor man for such a long time, and I truly regret it. I should have been thanking him for his selflessness every day, instead of only thinking the worst of him just because of how he looks. His size, brawn, and tattoos were all I saw, when all along he has the kindest eyes and most caring nature. Making the decision here and now, I swear not to judge him so harshly going forward and to make an effort to get to know the real him.

It's at that moment that I'm astonished to realise that I was talking to Hermes and laughing with him before, without any hesitation. For just a moment in time, I forgot to be afraid. I forgot that I was locked in a cage of my own making and actually laughed. And not just any laugh, but one with a giant Drake shifter all alone.

A tubby little hedgehog waddles over to my hand and sniffs the empty space, hoping to find a snack. I immediately pick up some of Hermes' pile of goodies and feed it to the spiky little dude.

"They like you," Hermes states quietly. "I'm glad. You know you can come out here any time you like. They'd love such pretty company. I'm sure they're sick of my ugly mug by now."

I like the idea of visiting my new little friends every day and smile at him. "Thank you, I'd like that," I say, conscious this time that I'm talking out loud.

We sit there in silence for a little while playing with the forest animals, and I steal a few secret glances at Hermes, watching delightfully at every sweet thing he does.

Unable to go a moment longer without apologising, I say with honest remorse. "I'm sorry that I've been so hard on you. You didn't deserve it, and I'll do better. I'm very grateful that you saved me and continue to keep me safe here." I can't look him in the eye when I say it, but I know that he can hear my sincerity.

I watch as Hermes goes to take my hand, pulling it back at the last second. He clears his throat. "You really don't have to apologise, little one. I know what I must look like to you," he says, his voice laced with a sorrow that I don't quite understand. Maybe I've hurt him with my fear more than I realised.

Being as brave as I can muster, I pat his knee, feeling him stiffen at the contact. "How about we be friends?" I ask, hopefully. "You seem to be the only person I have been able to talk to after all, and that's no small feat."

"I like your accent. It's different from what I've heard before," Hermes says happily.

"Thanks, I'm kiwi. Aotearoa is my home and I don't miss it as much as I'd like to if I'm being honest," I add, mournfully. "It's a beautiful place, but it's filled with bad memories for me, and I don't ever want to go back."

"You never have to." Hermes' voice is harder than I've heard today, and it makes me look up at his tight features. "You're safe here, and Rathe is your home now. I won't let anything or anyone hurt you again."

For some reason, I believe him; he seems like the kind of man that means what he says, and if he says he's going to protect me, then it means he believes that he can. I have seen his Drake, after all; I can't imagine anything beating him in a fight. Except perhaps Blayze, or Salvatore, but they're kind of my friends, and I don't think that they'd ever try to hurt me. Plus, Summer would make them pay for it if they did.

I chuckle quietly at the force that is my friend Summer; she's one hell of a woman, and it would take a lot to tear her down. I'm not surprised she has so many Kindreds, now that I understand how it all works here; it would take that many strong shifters to take on her kick ass attitude.

"What are you giggling at?" Hermes asks, getting up and dusting his bum off before reaching down for me.

I take his huge hand with my tiny one, awed at the size difference, and answer, "I was thinking about my friend Summer. Have you met her? She's a firecracker."

As Hermes pulls me to my feet as if I weigh no more than a

feather, he answers with a laugh, "Oh, I know her alright. She once threatened to whoop my ass, and all I was doing was helping her. She's a fine female. Very strong. Her males must be very proud to have such a spirited Kindred."

A sudden weight pushes on my chest, awareness of how little I have to offer my own Kindred when I find him, if I even have one. Especially now that I'm having another man's baby, it can't be a selling point. I am a lot of things, but strong isn't one of them. What if strength is what the men here look for in a good Kindred? Does that mean I'll never be accepted? Never be loved like Summer and Janice are?

The thought brings my mood right down, and I quietly excuse myself, leaving the befuddled Hermes behind as I practically run back to my room, letting tears flow unchecked from my eyes. I place my hand on my belly and think of my little bean, at least we have each other.

CHAPTER FOURTEEN

HAVANA

"Snap!" Hermes cheers happily, jumping out of his seat like a big kid, smiling from ear to ear. "I win again!"

I giggle at his exuberance. "You don't play games much, do you, mister?" I ask him, shaking my head.

"I don't know what you're talking about," he denies with a twinkle in his eyes. "You just feel bad being next to such an epic winner, admit it."

I laugh even harder. "That's gotta be it." I roll my eyes.

Matthew snorts unhappily, standing up and backing away from the table. "If you wanna stay here and endure his childish behaviour, that's on you. I'm outta here."

Hermes blows a raspberry at his retreating form, and I shake my head at him. "Seriously?"

With a shrug, he starts to shuffle the deck of cards in front of us, humming an unrecognisable tune, looking chuffed at his winning streak. It warms my heart to see him looking so happy. Since the day we made peace in the garden, Hermes has had a second wind at life, always laughing, smiling, and humming. It's beautiful and has cheered me up substantially.

It's nowhere near as often that I let myself slip into unhappiness if I can help it. The atmosphere in the house is just too uplifting to deny. The hardest time of the day is when I get into bed, hold my softly rounding belly, and remember how fleeting these happy days are. It won't be long till they realise I'm pregnant because at some point I'll be too round to hide it.

Brushing off the negative thought, I smile at my new-found friend and try to focus on right now, not wanting to ruin my rare good mood.

"So, what are you gonna do with me once your Kindred finds you?" I ask, not so innocently, fear of him turning me out, constant. "She might not appreciate me being in your home."

Hermes winks at me cheekily, "Don't you worry about that, little one, I'm sure she'll love you just as much as I do."

Even though I know his words are a joke, the L word has my cheeks heating. What must it be like to be loved by such a man? Hermes has grown exponentially in my thoughts of him, and I can only imagine how lucky a woman would be to have someone like him love them and care for them endlessly. He treats me amazingly, and I'm just a visitor in his home. Jealousy briefly visits me, but I refuse to let it take hold.

"She better because I quite like it here. I'll miss this place when I go back to Summer's pack," I say. "When is Blayze coming to get me, anyway? You said it wouldn't be too long, last time I asked."

Hermes stops shuffling and looks at me with a steady gaze. "Are you in such a hurry to leave?" he asks, and I could swear I heard hurt in his voice.

"It's not like that," I assure him. I think of bean growing inside me and hope that I can get out of here before he finds out about him. Summer would never let me be taken back to Leon, and if I'm being honest with myself, I don't want to see Hermes' disappointment with me. I don't think I could handle his rejection right now. "I just miss Summer, and I'm dying to meet Mina and Demetrius. If you remember, I was whisked away before I got a chance to see them."

Nodding in understanding, Hermes dishes out the cards, but his face remains sombre as he does so. "Are you gonna miss me, big fella?" I joke with him, but his eyes meet mine as he seriously replies, "More than you know."

My heart skips a beat at the intensity I find there, and I find myself shifting in my seat, an unexpected heat hitting me in places forever dormant.

Hermes looks down at his cards before his head snaps up to me, tilted to one side. "Are you okay?" he asks more huskily than normal.

I fold my curls behind my ears and squint at the cards in front of me, but I feel his eyes drilling into me.

"Do you have trouble seeing?" he asks suddenly. "You always squint, and sometimes it's like you don't see the things right in front of you." Hermes pulls at his beard in thought.

"I used to have glasses, but I lost them a long time ago when I was first taken by the six-pack," I explain. "I didn't want to complain because it's not like you can do anything about it."

Hermes' chair slides back, and he exits the room quickly without a word. Okay then. Within less than a minute, he returns with Scooby.

"Can you please get a Sorcerer from the closest village?" Hermes tells Scooby. "Tell them I'm happy to pay what's required, but that we need a female's vision repaired."

Scooby nods and looks at me. "What happened to your eyes?"

"I was born like this. I've always had bad eyesight," I tell Scooby before looking at Hermes. "You don't need to do that. I've learned how to deal with it and the headaches are pretty manageable."

"Headaches?" he asks grumpily, turning back to Scooby. "You'd better hurry up. I don't like the idea of her being in unnecessary pain. I'm happy to pay you for the extra assistance."

They give each other a look with a silent message that I don't understand, but Scooby bows slightly. "Not necessary. It's my pleasure to be of service. I'll be back by tomorrow, hopefully. I'll get them to transport us here."

With that, Scooby leaves the room and Hermes looks at me with concern. "I wish you'd told me earlier," he grumbles. "Although it's nice to hear your voice speaking to the others, and that you're comfortable enough to do it. You're safe here. None of us will hurt you. I know I say that a lot, but I know that you need to hear it."

Of course, he's right. Every now and then I find myself retreating into myself, and the bad memories of my life take over inch by inch. Having constant reassurance has helped, even though I technically shouldn't need it by now, but past trauma has a way of taking over when I least expect it.

Nighttime is a bitch because at first I can't sleep because of all my doubts and fears about what people are going to say about bean, and then when I do fall asleep I get bombarded with nightmares; both from my father and from my time with Leon.

Derryn and Matthew come into the room, and I can't help but notice the cheeky look on Derryn's face; his half smile a sure indication that he's done something mischievous.

"Your dinner's ready on the balcony," Derryn crows happily. "Made with love by yours truly. Enjoy, kids. Matthew and I are gonna go hunting for a couple of hours. Dinnae do anything we wouldn't do."

I scoff, "What, like using my manners at the table?" I joke back. He scarfs his food down like an animal, without even chewing.

"Har-dee-har," Derryn mocks. "And I went out of me way and everything. I see how it is."

He leaves the room moaning about how he's unappreciated, and Matthew follows him out, laughing at his ridiculous sook.

Hermes rises from his seat and holds out his hand for me. "Shall we?"

Smiling, I take it, and surprisingly he continues to hold my hand in his as he directs us to the balcony and the sight before me has me doing a double take. The table is decorated with rose petals, a bunch of red roses in a vase at the centre surrounded by short candles. The space around the table has four tall, large candleholders, setting the mood lighting perfectly.

I look at the plates piled beautifully with some kind of creamy pasta and two glasses of white wine. The smell of the meal wafts to me and makes my mouth water for a taste. Luckily, my morning sickness has tapered off to almost nothing, except for the smell of bacon. It still makes me puke every time it's cooked in the house.

"Wow!" I exclaim. "This all looks so special. What's the occasion?" I ask Hermes.

His face looks as shocked as mine, and I can tell instantly that he had no idea that the others were planning this. He looks at me and smiles softly. "You're the occasion."

I blush furiously at that and look down, unsure of how to take such an open compliment. It's not often that I've heard a man say something so flattering to me. Not without it being disgusting or highly inappropriate.

He pulls me over to a chair and pulls it back for me; I sit down, and he slides it in behind me like a true gentleman. I inhale the scrumptious scent of dinner as Hermes goes back inside. Not sure why he left, I fiddle with the cutlery beside my plate.

Returning with a fur coat, Hermes stands behind me and tenderly places it over my shoulders, careful not to touch my skin without my permission. He's always so thoughtful like that.

"Is that better?" he asks me softly, circling the table and taking his own seat.

I nod appreciatively and look back down at my plate with a newly ravenous hunger. "Eat, little one. That's why it's there," Hermes chuckles, picking up his own fork and digging in. "This is actually incredible. If I knew that Wolf could cook, I would've put him to work."

We both know it's a lie, though. Hermes seems to get great joy from cooking for everybody every day. I've offered to help out myself a few times now, but he won't have a bar of it. I can't even help with the dishes. The kitchen is very much his domain. I'm surprised he even let Derryn cook tonight.

A deep moan of ecstasy slips from my mouth as I devour my first bite. "Oh my gosh, that's divine," I say with a mouthful of food, completely forgetting my manners.

"I never get tired of hearing you moan when you eat," Hermes mutters, exhaling. "It's very hot, I'm not gonna lie."

I've never heard any of the guys here say anything like that to me before, and I choke on my food in surprise. Hermes scrunches his face and grabs the wine in front of me, trying to pass it to me. He clearly regretted what he said immediately, guilt is written all over his tattooed face.

I shake my head at the glass of wine and push his hand away, still coughing violently. Hermes looks confused, but runs off to the kitchen. Returning with a tall glass of water I happily take from him, sipping it until I calm down my coughing fit.

"Thank you," I get out, catching my breath.

"You don't like wine?" he asks, pointing to the untouched glass.

Obviously, I can't tell him I'm pregnant and can't drink it. I go for something that is still true. "My Dad was a drunk and not a very nice man, so I don't drink alcohol." I have had a couple of drinks in the past, and normally I'd be okay with one glass of wine, but I most certainly wouldn't drink more than that for fear of turning out like him.

My hand unconsciously lowers to my stomach, rubbing my little bean. *I'll be a good mummy, you'll see. I'm nothing like him. I'll never hurt you, baby.*

Hermes growls low and stuffs food in his mouth, clearly trying to hide his anger at my father, and it's kind of sweet that he cares enough to not only get angry on my behalf but also to try to hide it so that he doesn't scare me.

I lean over the table and take his hand in mine. "Thank you for being kind to me. It means a lot."

He turns his hand into mine, and we just sit together holding hands for a few minutes, enjoying each other's company before returning to our delicious meal that ended up being creamy chicken and avocado fettuccine. I devour the entire plate and bean must have loved it as much as I did because he never made me feel sick once. Success!

"As for Blayze coming," Hermes randomly says while I sit back, enjoying the food coma creeping up on me. "I got a message yesterday that Salvatore's coming instead, and he'll be here mid next week."

I feel his eyes on me and find him surveying my expression. "What's wrong Hermes?" I ask.

"You don't have to leave, you know," he says, almost pleadingly. "You're welcome to stay here with us, with me. This is your home as much as it is mine now."

His words touch me, and I'm surprisingly tempted to stay here because I feel at ease here in a way I never did with Summer's pack, but I have to think of bean and what's best for them. He won't want me here when he knows that I'm more trouble than I'm worth. "I appreciate it, but it's time for me to go home."

I get up and excuse myself for the night, wanting to get out of here before I start crying again. My hormones own me now, and I am their bitch.

* * *

"Noooo!" I scream, desperately pushing him off me. "Please!" I scream as loud as I can, needing it to stop. *Please, God, make it stop.*

I sit up in a cold sweat and search around me, desperate to find him, but realising that it was just a dream. I'm all alone in my safe room, and he can't get me here. Dad will never get me again.

My hands drop to my belly, and I start to sob at the memories bombarding me from my nightmare. The only time I fully remember what I've been through is when I wake up screaming. By morning, it will all be a haze again; my brain unable to hold on to it all for very long.

Smash!

My door bangs open and a crazed-looking Hermes stands in the threshold with his braids all over the place, his black underwear and tattoo covered body in full view, his large hands clutching his two axes tightly.

His eyes travel over the room intently, his breaths panting and eyes wild, clearly ready to fight off whatever intruder he finds.

"Where are they?" he growls low, looking at every inch of the room before stalking to my vast window and staring out of it. "Tell me, little one."

For the first time, he looks down at my shaking form, gripping my blanket to my chin, my face wet with the tears of my past visiting me. His face drops, and he steps towards me.

"Don't cry. It's alright, I'm here now. Just tell me where they are, and I'll make them go away," Hermes says softly, a pained expression at seeing my tears.

I shake my head and choke on a sob. "It's- it's no one," I sniff. "Just bad dreams. I'm sorry."

Hermes puts his axes on the ground and sits next to me on the bed, with his arms wide. "Come here, darling. I've got you."

Without thought, I crawl into his huge lap and let him hold me as I cry so hard that I have to gasp for air. It's been such a long time since somebody held me as I cried, and I really let myself feel the grief of my life.

Hermes softly coos in my ear and strokes my hair tenderly, telling me everything's going to be alright, and he'll never stop saving me, no matter what. And I believe him. His sweet caresses and selfless actions make me cry even harder. Why did I have to be pregnant? I could've had a life here with him.

He stays with me like that for what feels like hours, never complaining as I soak his bare chest with my sorrow. Eventually, I cry myself out, and he lays me down and tucks me back into bed, wiping my face down with a warm flannel.

"Sleep, little one," he tells me laying next to me on top of the blanket, "I won't leave, I promise."

I fall into a deep sleep with my head on his chest, and his arm around me, listening to the heartbeat of the sweetest man I've ever known. My last conscious thought, that I'm screwed because I now know that I love Hermes, but I'm leaving next week.

. . .

THE NEXT DAY a Sorcerer I've never seen before, Duff, comes over to fix my eyesight. Understandably, he makes me super nervous because the last time I met one of his kind; he helped Leon to kidnap me.

However, I am extremely relieved that not only does he keep as quiet as he can; he is also super gentle and patient with me. I'm assuming Hermes sat him down and put the fear of the Gods in him, if he upset me. I can't even be mad because I really need the gentle approach that I get.

Duff is from the village nearby and apparently helps as many Mhanu as he can. He doesn't even charge Hermes for his time because he is happy to help.

All Duff does is place his hand above my closed eyes without touching me. Beneath my lids I can kind of see a blue light and feel a small amount of heat, not even enough to be uncomfortable, and when he tells me to open my eyes, it's like seeing the world for the first time. The beautiful colours around me, vibrant and clear, and Hermes' face is beautiful in a whole new way.

Inside Hermes' glacial blue eyes is a twinkle of kindness that I wish I'd seen when we first met, because it's unavoidably there, and I hate that we've wasted so much time with me fearing him.

CHAPTER FIFTEEN

HERMES

Anxiety swirls in my stomach like a pack of rabid dogs threatening to make me chuck up my breakfast as I sit on the balcony waiting for Salvatore to arrive. He should be here any moment, and I have spare clothes waiting for him beside me in case he didn't bring his own. I have no doubt that he's flying here today; it's much quicker that way, and he won't want to be away from his babies for longer than necessary.

"Hermes?" Havana's quiet, husky voice says from behind me, bringing a smile to my face. "Why don't you wait inside with us? It's cold out here."

I turn with concern, looking at her exposed appendages. "Go back inside, little one. I don't want you to catch a cold. I assure you we don't feel the cold like you do, and I'm absolutely fine," I say, but still see worry in her precious little features. Gods, she *is* beautiful. "I need to wait here; it's polite to greet him as he arrives, but he won't be long, darling. Go inside now."

I can't believe I'm letting Salvatore come to my home and take her away from me. I swallow a growl that threatens to rip loose; the thought of Havana leaving me has my beast crying inside me and wanting to fight to keep her.

Maybe I should go with them? Just to make sure she gets there okay. Who am I kidding? I just don't want to leave her side. If I go with them, I'll never come back home and without a shadow of a doubt, I wouldn't regret it, but I have the distinct feeling that part of her wanting to leave is to get away from me.

We've become very close since that fateful day in my garden, and although I knew I wanted her before as my Kindred, now I'm hopelessly in love with her. She is by far the strongest, most incredible female I've ever known. All the things she's been through should have made her a shell of a person, but she fights for herself every single day. I see it in her eyes; I see it when she smiles and when she laughs. Havana is my whole world, and I don't know how I'm meant to go on without her. Maybe Salvatore will know what to do? He had to fight for his female too; I believe.

Speaking of, Salvatore's large, red and black dragon comes into view. He's a magnificent beast and one of the most impressive Dragons I've come across in Rathe, not that there's many left. Just like the Drake and Leviathan, the fire Dragons are rare these days. Not as rare as Phoenix and Griffins, but there's still a lot less of us than most.

With a low swoop of his wide wings, Salvatore lands and instantly shifts into his humanoid form. Jogging up the stairs, I throw the spare clothes at him.

"How's it going? Was the flight alright?" I ask, looking away and giving him privacy to dress. While we're used to nudity, it doesn't mean we have no manners.

Salvatore claps my shoulder once his clothes are on and answers in his usual gruff voice. "Good, friend. No issues at all."

"Good, good. Come on in. Havana has been looking forward to your visit for a while now," I tell him, leading him inside.

Salvatore clears his throat. "Visit?" he asks. "I had the assumption that Havana was coming back with me to our pack? Has the plan changed, and no one thought to tell us? Summer won't be happy about that. She's been dying to have her home."

In a quiet voice I say, "I'd like to talk to you about that later on, when we have a moment of privacy, if that's alright with you?"

Nodding in understanding, we move into the living room to a beaming Havana. "Salvatore! It's really you. How's Summer? How're the babies?" Havana all but gushes, coming over to him with a confidence that makes me proud to see. She's come so far in such a short span of time.

Salvatore's eyes widen, and he looks at me with a "What the fuck?" look, and I just shrug with a smile. Loving how shocked he is by her exuberant greeting.

"Look at you, female," Salvatore crows excitedly with his arms wide. "I barely recognise you with that huge smile on your face." Just as I expected, her cheeks pinken beautifully at his compliment. "Summer and the babes are doing great. They're all over the place now and unstoppable forces like their mother. It keeps us all very busy."

Even Salvatore has changed from the male I used to know; his smile was as rare as Havana's was, and look at him now, gushing over his kids with a grin that surprisingly suits him.

I want that.

Looking at Havana's belly, I can imagine her petite little body curved with my baby inside, filling her with hope and love. I would give anything to be able to share a life with her and grow our own family together. It's the kind of dream I gave up a long time ago, believing it would never happen for me, and now that my Kindred's in front of me, I don't know if I can give it up. I intend to fight for this female, and if I have to move to Salvatore's pack in order to court her, then so be it.

Tilting my head, I notice her stomach is a lot rounder than it was when she first got here, and I smile even deeper, knowing that I've fed her so well that her body's filling out. Her chest has also noticeably been growing larger, but I've made a point not to look, knowing she won't appreciate it.

"You look very healthy," Salvatore says, looking her up and down, but then his face scrunches in... concern. "You smell different. Are you pregnant? Nobody told me. Who's your Kindred?" His face brightens up again excitedly, and he turns to me. "Is that why you wanted to talk to me? Well, this changes everything." He looks between the other males and me, "Well, who's the lucky daddy?"

A sob rips from Havana's mouth, and one hand goes to her throat in clear panic, while the other one lowers to her small, round belly. *Oh, my Gods! She's pregnant?*

"I think you're confused," Matthew says slowly. "Havana hasn't touched anyone that I know of," and he looks at me questioningly. "I would've smelt it."

I shake my head. "I swear, I didn't touch her. This has to be a mistake."

Salvatore looks confused and stares down at Havana's shaking form. "Am I wrong?"

Another sob comes out, and Havana drops her face into her hands and starts to cry inconsolably. "I'm- I'm-," she chokes out, "sorry." And then turns and runs up the stairs towards her room.

I gaze at Salvatore, and his face fills with fury. "Are you telling me that none of you knew about this? How the fuck could you not know? I'll fucking kill that son of a bitch," he growls, his eyes turning a dark red.

At first, I don't understand what he's saying and then, *bang... bang... bang...* my heartbeat pounds against my chest and pure rage fills my veins, acid in my lungs.

I stumble outside, barely able to control my shift, and the second I get clear of the house, my body rips open, the beast emerging. My Drake tears into being with a roar of pain and visceral rage, unable to contain it a moment longer.

My Kindred was raped and impregnated by Leon!

I didn't protect her!

She was too afraid to tell me!

I will *kill him!*

He will die bloody, and I will gift her his heart and balls!

Another heart-wrenching roar pulls from me, blind fury taking over, and I run and run until I plough into the opposing hill, smashing through the earth like it's butter. Ripping it from the very ground it's a part of. Tearing and smashing. Growling and roaring. The pain of my failure to protect my Kindred enough to drive me insane. How could I leave her so long in his hands? How could he do this to my little one?

No wonder she fears me. I am a beast just like him, and she must think I will do the same thing, or worse.

I cry out, a wail that has all the wildlife fleeing, the birds flying away as fast as they can. Everything around me disperses at my Drake's cries of pain.

I failed her!

For longer than I'd like to admit, I roar and pummel; the emotions overwhelming me at Leon's betrayal of the female that owns my heart and soul, too much to take.

I collapse into the hole of sunken earth I created, shifting back and curling into a fetal position. My body is trembling with exhaustion.

Slow, heavy steps approach me, and I know it's Salvatore because the others wouldn't have the balls to come near me right now with my beast uncontrollable.

"I didn't know," Salvatore says quietly, throwing pants down to me. "I had no idea, or I would have brought it up differently. Derryn told me that she doesn't know about you. I think it's time you told her because right now the poor girl is bawling her eyes out in her bedroom, scared to death at your behaviour. The fear emanating out of her room has all the males pacing uncomfortably through the house. I know that this is fucking awful, but you have to get your shit together for that female, or I'm taking her today. She needs to be safe and feel it. Can you guarantee that you won't harm her because of this baby?"

Panting, I roll over to face him with a scowl. "Of course I won't hurt her. She's mine. She's everything." My voice comes out as broken as I feel, and Salvatore's eyes soften.

"Good. It's time to get up then. Rub some dirt in it and look after your female," he states, stalking off and leaving me in my own pit of despair.

Grabbing the pants, I slowly get dressed, my body aching because of how violently I rampaged. I take in my surroundings and am instantly guilty for ruining what was probably home for many of my woodland friends. I'll make an effort to make it up to them this week with treats and new shelters. The hill once here, now nothing more than a ditch of broken dirt.

I have a lot of making up to do. I think of the poor female that is probably hiding in her bed, terrified of me, and sigh deeply. We've come so far, and I think I just fucked it all up.

CHAPTER SIXTEEN

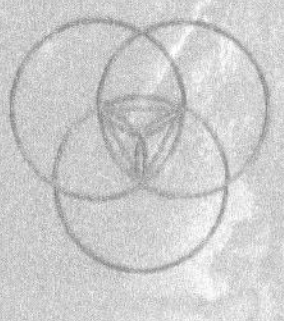

HAVANA

The bellow of outrage pouring from Hermes' Drake intensifies my sobs as I crawl under the covers of my bed, determined to hide from what's happening outside.

He knows.

How long before he changes back and throws me from his house? I visualize his disgusted face as he sneers down at me that I'm dirty and that he's taking me back to my owner.

Please, I don't want to go back there. Don't make me go back to him.

More roars of agony make the solid walls vibrate, and my whole body curls up and shivers uncontrollably with fear. Wrapping myself around my unborn baby in an attempt to save him from the horrors of the world.

They all know.

My gaze begins to darken, and I feel the familiar lull of my daze start to take over, protecting me from my fear, protecting me from the truth that I'm unwanted, soiled.

Relaxing, I let the darkness take hold of me and slip into the empty void of my own mind, disappearing down my very own rabbit hole of nothingness.

* * *

"Havana," a voice echoes from far away. "Havana, come back to us. Come on, female, you can do it."

Salvatore?

What's he doing here?

My eyes focus on his heavily bearded face as he kneels down on the side of my bed, his features tense with worry. *What's going on?* I look around the otherwise empty room and back at him.

"That's a good girl," Salvatore huffs out a relieved exhale. "You had me worried there for a little while."

Memories of my pregnancy being outed and Hermes' furious response trickles back, and I gasp, my hands covering my mouth. I guess my time here has come to an end. I'll always be haunted by the wailing of his Drake at the news of my baby. I knew he wouldn't be happy, but his response was way more severe than I was prepared for.

"It's okay. You're not in any danger. Slow your breathing down and focus on my words," Salvatore says to me slowly. "You're safe. Nobody's going to hurt you."

"Hermes?" I whisper.

"Do you want me to get him?" he asks and I shake my head rapidly. "Okay. Okay. He's fine and resting right now. I'm sorry that you had to hear that. He obviously didn't deal with the news very well. I can't speak for him or how he's feeling, but I can promise that he doesn't mean any harm to you."

Finding it hard to believe, I look away, but he grabs my chin so that I have to face him again. "He. Won't. Hurt. You. Hermes isn't mad at you Havana, babies are a gift here. He's angry at Leon for hurting you. For some reason, he hadn't thought of the fact that Leon may have... well, you know. It shook him to the core. He feels very protective of you, but if you don't feel safe here anymore, you are more than welcome to come home with me. You know you'll always be welcome with us and regardless of how this baby came into being, I'm very happy for you, and Summer will be too. You never know, that babe might just be the Kindred of one of ours."

I give him a small smile; the thought of my bean growing up with Summer's twins always makes me smile.

"There you go. That's the smile I wanted to see. Why don't you come down for dinner? Matthew's apparently serving pickled eel with rice," Salvatore says, and I screw up my face because that sounds disgusting. I've never liked eel, much to my dad's chagrin.

"No, thank you," I whisper.

"Did you want me to bring something up here for you? Anything you want. We have to keep that baby happy and healthy now, don't we?" he says, guilting me into eating even though I have no appetite whatsoever after today.

With a sigh, I ask for my normal pickles and tomato juice, and it's his turn to screw up his face. What can I say, bean loves it.

Salvatore gets up, and before he leaves the room asks me, "Do you want to come home with me tomorrow, or do you want to stay here? Tell me honestly, and there's no wrong answer. I'll support whatever you choose."

I think about it for a moment and picture Hermes' smiling face and soft humming and know if I leave, I'll miss him terribly, but I'm not sure if I'm welcome here anymore. I simply say, "I don't know."

* * *

HERMES

The ceiling above me is all I can stare at as my body lies heavily on my large, four-poster, hardwood bed; the weight of true regret caving my chest in. Between the guilt over not rescuing Havana in time and my violent outburst to what should have been good news, I'm mortified.

Poor Havana must have known this whole time. Her vomiting, tiredness, and weight gain all make sense now, and I feel stupid that I didn't figure it out earlier. I just didn't want to believe that Leon could hurt her like that. She's so innocent, so pure, and that animal took advantage of that. I have no doubt in my mind that he took her without her permission; her fear of being touched is obvious and no wonder.

Last night neither of us went downstairs. My focus was on any sound coming out of her room, the quiet tears she shed, not quiet enough for me not to notice. It brought silent tears to my own eyes, knowing that I'm the reason she's crying, and that I can't go near her right now to try to help.

I heard her go downstairs for breakfast about half an hour ago, and I've been putting off showing my face. But I'm not a coward, and it's time to face the music and apologise. It's a good sign that she was willing to go down, though. Maybe Havana can find it within herself to forgive me.

Standing up, I pull a clean shirt on and go down to join everyone else with my head held high and remorse in my eyes. I follow the voices into the dining room where everyone is chatting over a bowl of oatmeal, except the silent beauty at the end of the table, pushing around the mush mindlessly.

"Good morning," I announce, even though everyone but her would have heard me coming down the stairs.

Havana's shoulders tense at my words, and I inwardly curse myself for giving her a reason to react that way. I take a seat next to her but stare at my hands resting on the table. "I'm really sorry for what happened yesterday. It wasn't because you're pregnant; I just couldn't deal with," I swallow hard, finding it hard to mention Leon's name, "everything else." A cop out, I know.

She whispers, "Okay," and gets up, leaving her uneaten meal behind, disappearing out the front door, and I have to tell myself not to follow her out. Havana tends to go into the garden when she needs a break from everything, and I'm not going to take that sanctuary away from her now.

I sigh and plonk my head on the table in front of me.

"You fucked up, dude," Scooby points out unhelpfully. "Seriously, though, you've got some legit grovelling to do."

I look over and give him the stink eye; getting the hint, he shuts up and finishes his food.

"I think it's time for that talk now, buddy," Salvatore gruffly states. "How 'bout we head over to the living room while she's outside for some privacy?"

Agreeing, we both head to the room and sit on opposite large armchairs; both of us are units, so the size of the chairs are a blessing.

"You can't even look at her now, can you?" he starts, cutting to the chase. "That's not going to make her want to stay with you, and you know it. What are you going to do about this shit show you've gotten yourself into?"

Groaning, I rub my face vigorously. "I don't fucking know," I answer honestly. "I have no clue how I'm supposed to fix this. She wanted to leave here before my little episode. I can only imagine how fast she wants to get out of here now."

"You'd think so, but when I asked her last night if she wanted to leave with me, Havana said she didn't know." Salvatore's words shock me, and I look over at him with hope for the first time since yesterday. "Don't get too excited, dickhead. She sure as fuck isn't keen to stay either, no doubt. I think before all this shit happened, she developed feelings for your dumb ass. Gods know why with your ugly mug."

I lean back with an exhale. "I have no idea. Fuck knows, I don't deserve her. Do you have any advice?"

Salvatore scratches at his beard and runs his teeth over his bottom lip in thought. "Maybe if you tell her she's your Kindred, it might help. When Summer found out she was pregnant, she was fucking furious with us, but she forgave us without too much trouble. I didn't take her feelings into account at the time, truth be told, I was just ecstatic to hear she was expecting. Thinking back, I should have made more of an effort to see it from her point of view. Perhaps you should ask her how she's feeling about the whole thing. Havana's most likely terrified. Who knows what kind of scenarios are running through her head."

"When did you turn into such a soft spot?" I ask, amused by his new outlook on life.

The goofy as fuck grin he always seems to carry with him now shows up again. "Being a dad is better than I ever imagined, and we've been so fucking lucky to get a whole brood of awesome kids from Summer already. You should see our oldest twins; they're the cutest little girls and the eldest two blow me away; they're so smart and happy. Seeing Summer light up when she's surrounded by our kids is something else. I won't even get into how much those babies melt my fucking heart every time they smile at me, damn near kills me."

He stops for a moment and looks at me seriously. "You can have the same joy with Havana if you can fix this shit. That baby inside her is a fucking gift, and you're damn lucky that she has it. The biology behind that babe doesn't mean shit. My human kids are mine. I don't give a fuck that some dipshit donated sperm to give them life. I love each and every one of them as much as my own biological son. You hear me? If you're not willing to love that baby with every ounce of you, then let her come home with me, but if you're ready to jump into family life, fucking fight for it."

"Any child that comes from her will be loved by me, if she'll have me," I answer honestly, "but what if she doesn't want me in her life like that. What should I do?"

"Accept it. You can't force someone to love you, Hermes. All you can do is give her your best and hope it's enough," Salvatore answers.

"I'm going to let her decide for herself. I would hate to always feel like I forced her to stay with me over guilt or something like that. I want her to want to stay with me, to decide that I make her happy. I will give that female every piece of my heart and soul. If I'm honest with you, I already have," I announce sadly. "I can only pray that she chooses to stay."

Salvatore gets up and starts walking out, stopping beside me. With a hand on my shoulder, he says, "It's your choice, my friend. Good luck. I wish for you the same happiness that I've found." With a pat, he leaves me there to contemplate my fate.

The day passes slowly, and every time Havana and I are in the same room together, my guilt gets the better of me, and I can't look at her and see the pain clearly on her face.

Her tears have flown freely throughout the day, her wet cheeks and puffy eyes a constant reminder of my fuck up. The quiet sobbing coming from her room between meals is enough to make my heart break over and over again.

Just when I get the courage to confront her with a better apology than my last pathetic one, I look through the small opening of her bedroom door to find her packing a small bag, filling it with the things I've given her since she came to live with me, and my stomach plummets.

She's leaving me. She's truly leaving me.

Helpless and scared, I stumble back to my own room and drop to my knees behind the closed door, silent tears coursing down my stubbled cheeks and soaking my beard. *What have I done?*

CHAPTER SEVENTEEN

HAVANA

I fold another dress into my small backpack, sniffing through my never-ending tears. I can't believe how hard this decision is. I knew that my feelings for Hermes have grown to love, but I stupidly thought that I'd be able to make this choice rationally when the time came, but now that I'm finally leaving, my heart feels ripped in two.

I shouldn't be letting it get to me, after all, Hermes thinks I'm so disgusting now that he can't even look at me. Every time I try to face him again, he looks away and refuses to even glance my way.

Bile rises in my stomach, threatening to make me sick again. I've already vomited three times today because of my emotional turmoil, and the stress of all of this can't be good for bean.

Taking a deep breath, I try to calm myself down again. *I've got this. I can get through this.* My chant of the day as I force myself to cope with what's happening and not shut down. I have to be present no matter what the world throws at me. I'm going to be a mother, and I can't daze anymore. What if my baby needs me and my mind shuts down? I can't do it; I just can't.

I straighten my spine and suck in my next round of tears, refusing to let them fall. *We've got this baby. I've got you.*

It's best if I leave, anyway; I can't have my baby in a place where it's not wanted. Salvatore made it clear that no one would ever make me go back to Leon, and that they'll do whatever it takes to continue to protect me and my unborn baby for as long as they need to.

I would never put bean through the stress of being around Hermes if he doesn't want him here. No matter what my feelings are for him, my child is more important, and he'll always come first, no matter what. I will take care of my baby's needs in a way that was denied to me growing up; he will only know love, kindness, and acceptance. If it means I have to be alone forever, then so be it.

An unexpected knocking at my door gets my attention and Matthew slowly opens it, reminding me that in my haste, I didn't close it properly when I came in.

"Do you mind?" Matthew asks at the threshold to my room, and I shake my head, waving my arm for him to enter.

"Thank you for getting me out of that place, Matthew. I'm really sorry that I didn't tell anyone about the baby, but I didn't want to be taken back," I admit.

Matthew strolls over and sits at the end of my bed, playing mindlessly with the strap of my bag. "We'd never do that to you, but I understand your hesitation. Why none of us thought of it as a possibility is on us. I think it was just a mutual understanding that we didn't want to believe that you'd been through something like that. It's hard to wrap our heads around any male wanting to do that to a female. I know their faction is so different from ours, but it's times like these that make it clear just how different we are. I'm sorry that he ever laid a hand on you, but I'm not sorry that you have the gift of life inside you, and I wanted you to know that if you ever need me, no matter where you are, I'll be there for you."

"Thank you. That means a lot. You don't think less of me?" I ask, my head lowered and ashamed.

His hand grabs mine and tugs lightly to get my attention, and I look at his face to find sadness in his eyes. "Never in a million years. This isn't on you. Nothing that another person does to you is *ever* your fault. It's a reflection of them and how good or evil they are, and there's absolutely no way that you're at fault for what that disgusting pig did to you. Don't you forget it. You're a gem in a world of stones; don't let their brand of filth dull your shine because you're one of a kind and perfect just the way you are."

A rogue tear breaks through my barrier, and I wipe it away. "I needed to hear that today." My lip trembles from the force of emotion ignited inside me at his words. No matter how much I logically know that I didn't deserve it, there's always a part of me that wonders what I must have done. Where I went wrong for people to hurt me the way they did. First my very own father, a man that's meant to protect me, and then a stranger who took me for the very reason to hurt me. It has to be me.

"I mean it," Matthew reiterates, perhaps seeing the doubt in my gaze. "It's not your fault."

I sit down beside him heavily, repeating inside my head, *it's not my fault. It's not my fault. It's not my fault.* Until I almost started to believe it.

Matthew puts my bag on his lap and bites his lip. "So, you've decided to leave, then?" he asks oddly and I nod, staying silent. He clears his throat, and I look at him. "There's something that I think you should know before you make your final decision to leave."

"I already have," I deadpan, not wanting to deal with more than I can handle right now.

"I know. It's just," he pauses and looks at the open doorway before turning back to me, his voice lower than before, "it's not right that you don't know. I'll probably get the shit beaten out of me for telling you something that's not for me to say, but you *have* to know."

I wave him on, knowing that he's not going to stop staring at me weirdly until I let him.

Relaxing his shoulders, he leans forward and almost whispers, "It's Hermes. I don't think he'll survive you leaving; I've never seen him so low, and I'm worried about what he's going to do when you leave. He's a good male, and it would kill me to know I could've saved both of you a lot of heartache by just speaking up."

"He hates me now, Matthew. If anything, he's probably counting down the minutes until I leave his house. He won't even look at me," I explain. "I thought... Well, I thought that I loved him, but it's different now. Everything has changed."

Matthew jolts to a standing position, his face alight with hope. "You love him?" he cries way too loud for my liking.

"Shush it, Matthew. I told you that in confidence, and shouldn't have said anything to you at all," I grumble, zipping up my discarded bag.

Matthew snatches it from me with a big smile. "Don't you see? You can't leave now. You're made for each other." I shake my head at him and try to get my bag from him, but he raises it in the air too high for me to reach.

"Give it back. This isn't a game. I'm leaving, and I'll go with or without that bag." I stand my ground with my hands on my hips. Jeez, this baby is giving me all sorts of confidence, but Matthew feels like the annoying little brother I never had.

"Havana." Matthew's voice goes low again, but the cheerful lilt is still very much there. "He's not hiding from you. He loves you, and he's ashamed that he didn't protect you from Leon. Don't you see? He feels like he failed you when he was meant to protect you."

I snort. "That doesn't make any sense. He didn't even know me before you guys found me. How could he have known to protect me, and why would it all be on him?" I'm getting grumpy from his ridiculous rantings. "As if Hermes' problem is that he didn't find me in time. Leon was on me almost instantly; there's nothing he could have done about it."

"You don't understand," he moans in annoyance. "You're his, he will always feel responsible for your pain."

"His? What the heck are you on about?"

Matthew drops the bag unceremoniously on the ground behind him and guides me to sit back down on the bed, kneeling in front of me with a wide grin. "You're his Kindred. He knew it the moment he saw you at Leon's village, but you were so scared of him, he didn't want to upset you. He's been moping around this place pining for you since you got here, and only after you stopped reeking of fear every time he was around did he start smiling again."

I stare at him, dumbfounded. There's no way he's telling the truth, but his eyes are shining with honesty, pleading with me to hear him.

"You're his everything, and hearing what Leon did to you damn near broke him. He feels responsible and unworthy of you. That's why he can't look at you, and now he's heartbroken because you're going to leave him because he fucked up," Matthew explains.

My mouth works like a goldfish out of water as I struggle with what to say or even think. *Kindred? No way! Holy moly.*

"Seriously?" I ask, astonished and... elated. Warmth heating up my cold heart and giving it another reason to pump.

Matthew nods, "Seriously. If you leave now, it will destroy him and if you love him still, it'll destroy you as well."

I jump up excitedly, knocking Matthew on his ass accidentally, but he laughs it off.

"Well, what are you waiting for? Go and get your male," Matthew says, laughing on the floor.

It's time to find out if he'll have me just the way I am, baby and all.

CHAPTER EIGHTEEN

HAVANA

Knocking on Hermes' bedroom door, I wait impatiently for him to answer, bouncing from foot to foot, determined not to let my nerves get the better of me.

With no answer, I cautiously open it, calling his name. Only silence returns my calls when I step inside his vast private domain. The large interior furniture shouldn't have shocked me because of his size, but the impressive, solid, dark wooden framing of his four-poster bed had my jaw dropping. All the matching furnishings are just as amazing, catching the level of detailing on each piece, making it clear that they were done painstakingly by hand.

Crossing over to his open balcony doors, I step outside and gaze out to the open plain beyond, the unexpected vision of Hermes' Drake pacing back and forth greeting me.

His behemoth beast is truly a sight to behold. The creature before me is so similar to a Dragon, except for the lack of wings and thicker, more muscular body mass. Hermes' legs resemble four sturdy tree trunks as he strides back and forth, shaking his humongous horned head; his lengthy spiked tail swishing around with what seems like irritation.

As I take him in with awe, it occurs to me with understandable surprise that he doesn't scare me. I'm looking at him in his more primal mode, and all I feel is fondness and love, not one ounce of fear or apprehension, and I can tell the moment the last bit of me holding back from him dissipates.

My heart filling with joy for the first time in forever, I turn back into the room, all but jogging to the stairwell and down.

I wish I'd never wasted so much time fearing him and pushing him away. The pain I've inadvertently given him since I've been here with my behaviour is regrettable.

Low mewling sounds fill the air, spurring me on faster. The sad longing of the cries coming from Hermes' beast, breaking my heart. All the times I caught Hermes staring at me with longing make sense now, and the memory of me constantly turning away from him has me sucking in a small sob.

I'm so sorry. I didn't know. I couldn't see through my fear.

Pushing open the front door, I bound down the steps towards the grassy plain beyond, Hermes' melancholy cries resounding.

The determination I feel should shock me after years of numbness and resignation to my fate, but everything about this feels right. All I can do is hope — the dangerous, dreaded thing in my life — that he'll accept me as I am.

Will Hermes want me now that he knows I'm having another man's baby, or will he want me to get rid of it? My pregnancy may not have been asked for, but bean is a part of me now, and I desperately need Hermes to be okay with him.

I approach his Drake and pause before him, waiting. I'm not really sure what I'm waiting for exactly, but I know that it's important for him to see me here. To know that I've come for him. What he does with that information is his choice, I suppose.

Knowing that the only way for him to talk to me is if he shifts, I ready my mind for his possible nakedness and decide that I'm going to be okay with it.

Hermes won't hurt me, that much I know now.

HERMES

Pain rips me inside out.

Unable to stay inside hearing Havana pack her bag ready to leave me behind, I came out here to let my Drake side take over, even though the visceral ache only intensified once I shifted.

The somber mewling of my beast is unavoidable, the sounds escaping me like the soundtrack of my agony.

Turning to pace back again, I come to an immediate stop, finding my ethereal Kindred standing in the middle of the path I'd made from my heavy gait.

What is she doing here?

Havana must have come to say goodbye.

A long, pained sound spews from my throat, unchecked. *Will this be the last time I see her? Will she miss me at all?* Another crippling cry escapes me.

I would do anything she asks me to, if she will just stay with me. I want Havana, and I want her baby; the mini Havana living inside her. I know that with everything she's been through, she might never have want of a male's body in the normal way again, and that's okay. I would never expect that from her. All I want is for her to let me love and worship her the way she deserves. I want to be the father that she needs for her unborn baby. I wish she could see that I only want her to be happy and safe.

Deciding not to be a coward, I start to shift back, hoping that my nakedness won't upset her, but sure that she must have understood what me shifting means by now. If she wasn't okay with it, she wouldn't be here.

I let the change take over and exhale in defeat. I don't want to say goodbye. Not yet, not ever.

Please, little one, let me love you.

CHAPTER NINETEEN

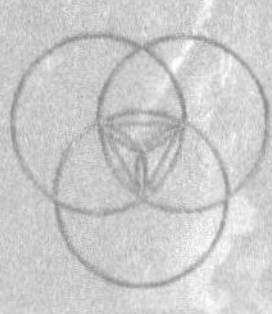

HAVANA

I stare in fascination at his diminishing form, the human frame coming forth. The strangeness of seeing something so grandiose, turning into a mere man in seconds, will always confound me, I'm sure.

Hermes stands tall with his head held high, and his ridiculously impressive body taut, as if he's ready for me to punch him. When in reality, it's more likely that he thinks I'm saying goodbye, inflicting what must be worse pain.

I've learnt since being in Rathe how exceptional the bond is between Kindreds and what it must mean to lose one. The agony is undoubtedly unbearable.

I raise my hands up in a defensive pose and tell him, "Hermes, we need to talk."

With a swift nod, he parts his legs and covers his junk the best he can under the circumstances, and I stifle a giggle, purposely looking at his eyes, so that I don't accidentally get an eye full.

Even with pained eyes, Hermes smirks slightly and asks, "Do you want me to turn around?"

I squeak, "No." Knowing full well that I can't stare at his ass for the whole conversation. "I'm okay."

Obviously not believing me, he raises an eyebrow at me, but I smile in return, determined to be a grownup about this. Nudity is normal for shifters and I will learn to deal with it.

"You didn't have to come out here just to say goodbye. You could have waved at me from the door," Hermes says through gritted teeth, his eyes filled with sorrow.

I step towards him, and he tenses even harder. "I didn't come here to tell you I'm leaving Hermes. I came to tell you that I don't want to."

Hermes sucks in a breath and holds it for what seems like way too long. Discomfort at this lack of breathing has me crying out, "Breathe, please." And he exhales a slow, deliberate breath, eyes never leaving mine.

"What do you mean, you don't want to?" he asks.

I lower my hands and tilt my head to the garden near the house. "Walk with me?" I ask. I take off my sweater and throw it at him. "Maybe tie this over your front so I can focus."

Looking somewhat relieved, he puts it over his front, tying it behind him. "I suggest you don't walk behind me then," Hermes recommends, hiding any smile.

I notice that a lot of the tension he was holding onto before has released considerably, obviously eager to know what I'm trying to say to him.

Stepping beside me, we begin to stroll towards the garden we both love so much, and I reach out and take his giant hand into mine. His step falters for a minute in shock before squeezing my hand in return.

For a moment, we walk in silence, just holding each other's hand and enjoying each other's company.

Breaking our comfortable silence, I say, "I have to tell you some things that I normally wouldn't say, and I need you to just listen." I sigh deeply, gathering all of my bravery. "When I'm done, I want you to answer my questions. Can you do that?"

"Whatever you need, female," Hermes replies softly, rubbing his thumb over the back of my hand.

"I've had a really tough life, and that's why I am the way I am. I know I'm not an easy person to get close to, but there's a reason for that, and it's essential that you understand me better if I'm going to choose to stay here, instead of going back to Summer," I start, sitting on a stone bench looking into the garden.

Hermes silently sits next to me, still holding my hand, so I continue, "My mum died when I was very little. She was a great mum from what I remember, but my memories of her are limited. Not long after she died," I pause, focusing on my breathing, "my dad started abusing me. I won't go into detail because I don't think I can, to be honest, and I don't want to, but I'm sure you can use your imagination. He abused me mentally, physically, and," I clear my throat, "sexually."

Hermes' entire body gets tight, and I can practically feel him vibrating from anger, but I keep my gaze towards the garden ahead of me, unable to look him in the eye.

"This happened my whole life until I was taken and woke up in Threshold; in a glass cage. And honestly, I hadn't felt that safe in a long time." I decide to be as honest as I can be, not wanting to ever have this conversation again. "I never thought of it as being locked up; it felt more like it was keeping the bad out. None of the men came anywhere near me, barely any of them tried to talk to me or even noticed me half the time."

"I never left my cell, except for really quick showers when nobody was around. Then overnight I woke up to this beautiful blonde lady staring down at me in a wooden cabin, and the first thing I thought was that we were being taken back home, and I was absolutely terrified. Thankfully, Summer explained where we were and what was happening pretty quickly."

"I know that most people would freak out over being in some weird other world, but for me, it was the best thing I'd ever heard, and I swore to myself that I'd never go back. There's nothing back on earth for me but misery. Summer, Bell, and Janice took me under their wing, never forcing me to become someone I'm not, and they accepted me just the way I was. I never had to reach too far out of my comfort zone because they were always there to help me and talk for me when I couldn't do it for myself. While I'll be forever grateful, since being here with you and the others, I've learnt how to speak for myself, and how to know the difference between a man who wants to hurt me and a man that doesn't."

I look at him, and then I find Hermes studying my face. A single tear slips down my cheek, and I wipe it off with my spare hand. "When I was taken again by the six-pack, I couldn't believe my luck. It felt like all the worlds were out to get me, and that there was nowhere I could hide from people wanting to tear everything I had left inside apart. The bad Bear man that took me only hurt me sometimes, which was a slight relief, but when they threw me into the market's dungeon and explained what was happening, I couldn't take it anymore."

"Time elapsed for me differently from there. I've always gone into what I call a 'daze' when I'm confronted with abuse of some kind, but it became my main way of surviving after a while. The time with Leon was the worst it's been since being back on Earth.

His constant visits undid my mind bit by bit. Verna, his mother, tried to bring me back whenever she could to get me to eat and wash, but I honestly have no idea how much time I spent there. It could've been weeks, months, or years for all I know."

I rub my aching temples, my head pounding with pain from the memories. "Leon came to me from the very first day, reigniting my distrust for men. I found myself wishing that the daze would come over me and swallow me whole. I didn't want to wake up anymore; I didn't want to remember, but Verna wouldn't let me go. I owe my life to her because without her, I wouldn't be sitting with you today, feeling real happiness for the first time since my mother held me."

Hermes squeezes my hand again, remaining silent, showing his ongoing support. "Thank you, Hermes, for showing me it's okay to hope again. I never thought I'd be able to, but here I am; hoping. I know I never asked for this baby, but he's everything to me now. He's the reason I fight every day to be stronger than the day before, because my baby will need me to be strong for him and speak for him until he can speak for himself. I need you to understand."

I turn to my side, taking both of his hands in mine and pulling them to my stomach. "I am a package deal, Hermes. I come with heavy baggage, a past that will never heal, trauma that will always be a part of me, and a baby that I already love more than life. Matthew told me that I was your Kindred."

Opening his mouth with a frown, I shush him before he can say a word. "I'm not done talking," I state with confidence, and proud of myself for that. "You should have told me yourself, if it's true, that is. Regardless, it's important that you know who I am and what's important to me. Wherever I choose to live, I need to be supported and understood because I refuse to live half a life anymore. I owe it to Bean to do better, to accept better. Now tell me, am I your Kindred, or was Matthew lying to me to get me to stay?"

Hermes lifts both of my hands to his lips and kisses them, his eyes never leaving mine. "You are mine, little one. I knew it the moment I saw your sad face in the window of that tower," he admits, with his heart in his eyes. "I should have told you, but you were so frightened of me. I didn't want to upset you."

Knowing he was right, I say, "That makes sense at the beginning, but what about later? I thought we were becoming close. Why didn't you tell me then?"

"I don't know. I guess by then *I* was afraid. I didn't think I could handle you rejecting me. I learned to love you as more than just my Kindred but as a female of worth," Hermes says.

"Do you want me?" I ask.

"Very much."

"What about my baby Hermes? Will you treat him badly because of where he came from?" I need to know, and whether my heart likes it or not, his answer will decide if I stay or if I go.

* * *

HERMES

The pounding of my heart pushes against my chest with intensity. *How is this happening right now?*

"Darling, I love every single part of you, especially your baby," I truthfully tell her, wanting nothing more in this world than to keep them both by my heart forever and a day. "You're everything to me, and if you'll have me, I'd love to be the father of this baby." I place my hand on her small, curved belly, love for them both overwhelming me. "Nothing would honour me more."

Havana sucks in a breath, and unshed tears fill her beautiful eyes. "Do you really mean that?"

"With all my heart," I say. "I'm so sorry about your past, and I wish I could rip the head off the man who called himself your father. That man is not your dad, Havana. No real dad would do that to his daughter. I knew that Earth could be barbaric, but I had no idea that people were that bad. Why did nobody help you?" I focus on keeping my anger contained, knowing that now is not the time.

Havana pushes her fingers through her wild mane of hair and looks out at the tranquil garden around us. "I had no one else, and I lost my voice. I was taught to stay quiet from a young age and one day, I just couldn't remember why I ever talked before. Nobody ever really hears people when they speak, they just hear what they want to."

I grab her chin gently and turn her back to me. "I swear to all the Gods that I will always hear you, Havana, even when you lose your voice."

Her tears slip free at my words, and I know I've touched her heart, like she's touched mine. "Do I have any chance with you? Do you think you could learn to love a man like me? I will never ask anything of you but your time and maybe one day your heart. I know you've been through a lot, more than I realised, and I would never expect *that* kind of thing from you, little one. You are enough, just as you are, and this child can be all we need, if you'll have me."

Footsteps approach us, and we turn to see Salvatore entering the garden with a guarded look on his face. "Sorry to intrude, but if you're coming with me, Havana, then we'll have to get going. I've got a long flight ahead of me."

Havana looks at me and then back at Salvatore with a smile.

"Sorry, but it looks like you're going home alone. My Kindred here is going to show me how to cook tonight. Aren't you?"

Unable to contain my excitement, I jump to my feet, lifting Havana into my arms and twirling her around. With a delighted squeal, she laughs joyfully, and I holler a "Whoop" into the air.

Salvatore claps his hands together and whistles happily for us.

"Your wish is my command, Kindred," I announce, wanting to kiss her soft full looking lips, but I refrain, not knowing if that's too far.

Havana reaches up and touches my bearded cheek softly, her eyes glittering with emotion. She gently tugs on my beard, bringing my face down to hers before leaning in and ever so lightly brushing her lips against mine.

The contact sends tingles through me, and it takes everything I have to remain still and let her sample me on her own terms. With a little more pressure, she kisses me properly but quickly, backing away with red-hot cheeks, her eyes darting away but a small smile on her cherry lips. It's more than I ever expected from her, and it's a gift I'll always remember.

I turn to see that Salvatore has left us alone in our special moment, and I'm grateful to know such a worthy male.

Taking Havana's hand, we head back towards the house; our house. I can't wait to share every day with her for as long as she'll have me. A dark shadow creeps into my mind, telling me that without claiming her fully she will die long before I do, but I brush it away, willing to enjoy every year that she has. When the time comes, I'll happily follow her. My life has been long and without her, it would be empty.

CHAPTER TWENTY

HERMES

It's been two weeks since my precious Havana decided to let me into her heart, and it's been the best two weeks of my life. I can't help thinking about how lucky I am as I watch her setting the table, humming a low tune as she goes.

The others have been suspiciously absent lately, and I have no doubt it's to give us room to bond together without interruption, and I'm super grateful for it.

"Come fly with me. Let's fly, let's fly away," Havana sings softly, not realising that I'm leaning on the door frame behind her, smiling widely. I have no idea what song this is, but she seems to like it a lot.

Turning around towards the kitchen behind me, Havana squeaks in surprise. "Sorry, darling, I didn't mean to startle you," I chuckle low, stepping forward and taking her hand into mine. "You have a beautiful voice, you know."

She waves her spare hand at me dismissively, accepting my big hand with her other one. "Don't be silly." Havana's warm brown cheeks flush red, giving her a soft glow.

"What's for dinner?" she asks, changing the subject. "Are the guys joining us tonight?"

The way Havana says that makes my heart soar, like she knows this is her house as much as it is mine. "I'm not sure. Do you want me to ask them to sit with us?" I ask happily.

Getting on her tiptoes, she grabs my shoulder to pull me down to her, and I instantly bend for her. With a gentle kiss to my bristly cheek, she smiles at me sweetly, and says, "Yes, please. I feel like I haven't seen them in days. It'd be nice to hear you all laughing together."

"Your wish is my command," I reply, placing my hand on her little belly. I love how it's slowly feeling more round and less like bloating. "Are you feeling okay? Is there anything you need?"

Havana puts her own hand on top of mine. "We're fine. Thanks for asking. Now go and get the others. I'll add more table settings."

Turning away from her, I smile stupidly as I walk out the front door, knowing I'll find Derryn, Matthew, and Scooby at the fire pit nearby. The smoke above it is a dead giveaway.

Matthew's hyena laugh has me chuckling when I approach the little get together. "Are you sure you're an Owl, because that laugh you've got there says otherwise," I say in greeting, and Derryn and Scooby laugh hard at the unfortunate truth of what I said. It's an atrocious laugh.

"Shut up you. I don't sound like a hyena," Matthew snorts in annoyance, his laughter snuffed out.

I scoff and say, "Never said that. You did. I take it I'm not the first one to tell you how ridiculous you sound?"

With a swift move of his hand, Matthew flips me the bird, and the others laugh even harder.

"Dinnae ken how Matthew's gonna get a Kindred with that cackle," Derryn chuckles. "What you doing with us anyway, when you've got a lass at the house keening for you?"

"Havana wanted me to invite you lot up for dinner. She's missed your company," I tell them and tack on as a joke, "I guess I wouldn't mind either."

Matthew gets to his feet immediately and claps his hands together. "Don't have to tell me twice."

"How's it all going with her, anyway?" Scooby asks me as we stroll back to the house. "You don't scent of her much yet." Hinting to the fact that we haven't had sex yet.

I clear my throat and answer, "It's not like that with us. I'm going to be the kind of male she needs, and that kind of thing is not for her. Our bond is stronger than that, and I'm fine with it."

"Are you pulling my leg?" Derryn asks incredulously, eyes as wide as saucers. "You've got to be taking the piss. How the feck are you meant to claim her if you don't get up in there?"

"Charming Derryn," Matthew says, screwing his face up. "I'm sure she'd appreciate that terminology."

Derryn scoffs. "I don't care what you call it, how's Havana meant to get claimed by you as your Kindred, if you don't do 'that kind of thing'." He uses his fingers to quote me. "Leon can take her back technically if she's not claimed, and you know it. And not just him, may I add. There's a lot of sick feckers out there, just waiting to knick off with an unclaimed female."

Matthew stops abruptly in front of us at the bottom of the front door steps, looking up nervously. Following his eyes, I spot a surprisingly pale Havana at the top, having clearly heard some of our conversation and not liking where it went.

I raise my hands defensively. "I told them we're not like that, little one. Please don't panic, everything's fine, I'd never pressure you." I walk up the stairs to her, stopping two below so that we were closer in height. "I love us just the way we are. Ignore them, they think with the wrong head."

Havana slowly shakes her head at me. "Is he telling the truth?" she asks, her hand tightly pressing on her belly. "Can I be taken even though I'm your Kindred?"

"You won't be, love. I'll protect you," I promise, taking another step, reaching out for the hand on her belly and taking it into mine.

One of the males behind me exhales a long, purposeful breath, clearly unhappy with my half-truth. But it's not a lie to me because I will protect her. The rest is irrelevant.

Havana, however, notices the discomfort between us and looks over to whomever it was and demands, "Explain. What isn't he telling me?"

My shoulders slouch, not wanting to have this conversation because I know it will make her uncomfortable and feel pressured when she shouldn't. No female should ever feel pressured for something, and especially not my little one. She's experienced enough of that for a lifetime.

"Please don't," I plead with her, but she doesn't look at me, her gaze focused on what I now realise is Matthew when I turn to check. *Fuck. Matthew is always honest because he's a worthy male.*

Matthew looks between me and Havana and gives me an apologetic look before stating, "You haven't technically been claimed yet, Havana. Hermes didn't tell us that. It's something we can scent, and it's clear that it hasn't happened yet. We're not the only males who will figure that out really quickly, and until you are claimed by a Kindred, you will be a target to any male with ill intentions." He scratches behind his ear uncomfortably and continues, "I'm sorry. I know it's none of our business, but I don't really see what the problem is. I know you've had a bad history with Leon, but Hermes is your Kindred; he'll never hurt you."

Squeezing my eyes tightly closed at his thoughtless words, I cringe and turn back to Havana, afraid of what I might see in her eyes. Opening them, I take in her tightly wound body, tense neck muscles and wide, scared eyes. I wish to all the Gods that they'd just kept their mouths shut. I hate nothing more than seeing Havana hurting and scared.

Havana's hand drops from mine and my stomach drops. "Don't listen to him, darling. You're safe with me, and we're good just the way we are. You don't need to worry about things like that, it's no good for our baby."

She sucks in a breath and whispers, "Our?"

It takes me a moment to figure out her confusion, and then I smile in realisation. "Of course *our*. This baby became mine the second you accepted me as yours, and I'll keep you both safe. Now and forever, I promise."

Havana's body visibly relaxes, and she looks back at Matthew with a tight smile. "Thank you for telling me, but I trust Hermes, and know that he won't let anything happen to us." She pats her baby bump. "Now come inside out of the cold, dinner's ready."

I watch her with pride as she walks back inside. Havana has come so far since we found her; she's so far out of her shell and blooming more every day. When once she sat in silence, shivering at each sound, Havana now holds her head up high, confident enough to tell me off when I put my feet on the table. When I'm really lucky, I even get to steal an odd kiss of her soft lips without a flinch, but instead a smile. I'm a lucky male to have found such a strong female.

While I happily accept that her body will never be mine to possess the way I dream of every night, I just make sure to ease my longing in the shower every morning, with visions of her soft body above mine. It's enough for me to take care of myself, and I swore to never pressure her, regardless of the fact that she's the most desirable female I've ever laid eyes on.

I shake my head at the wandering thought, as I watch her tight round ass walk away and a heavy hand lands on my shoulder. I turn to see Scooby shaking his head at me.

"You are one strong male if you can deny yourself like this, especially since it's obvious that you want her," he says, nodding at my crotch, and I look down mortified to see evidence of my previous thoughts, straining against my pants.

"Shit." I cover myself and breathe a sigh of relief when Havana disappears around the corner.

Derryn walks past and says quietly, "Go take care of that. I'll help her dish up dinner and say you had to go to the little lad's room."

Grateful for his idea, I swiftly stalk inside heading straight for the stairs, because he's right, if I don't take care of this now, it'll keep 'popping up' during our meal and that's the last thing I need right now.

"WHY DO you keep saying *he* when you talk about the bairn?" I hear Derryn ask Havana as I approach the dining room after discreetly taking care of my not-so-little issue.

Her sweet, low, raspy giggle floats through the doorway, and I walk in to see her face beaming with that blinding smile that I'll never get used to. "Well, I've been told how Mina's birth was a rare occurrence in Rathe because she's a girl. So, I assume it's most likely a boy in my belly, and I'm fine with that. I don't really mind either way, but I doubt that another girl will be born so soon."

Havana shrugs, obviously fine with whatever sex the baby is, but she's right. It was surprising for everyone when we heard about the birth of the Phoenix female. Obviously because of Mina's gender, but also because no one can remember the last time a female Phoenix was born. Usually on the odd occasion that a Phoenix gives birth, it's to a boy, and they breed with human females. The legend is that in ancient times, the females were too powerful for the Celestials to keep under their thumb, so they made it impossible for them to continue being born. Yet, Mina is alive and well, and a Phoenix for certain.

Havana's eyes meet with mine, and my heart melts a little. I can't believe my luck at finding her, and I can't wait to be a father. I'll do everything in my power to be the best dad I can be, and I'll teach him to cook and tend to the garden and surrounding animals. Of course, I will make it my duty to teach my boy how to fight, not just in his Leviathan form but also as a male, with axe in hand and courage in heart. He will be a fine boy because he'll have his mother's heart, of that I'm sure.

"Come and sit down, Hermes," she tells me kindly. "Your dinner's getting cold, and it's delicious. I was going to wait for you, but once it was in front of me, I kind of devoured it. Sorry."

Scooby laughs. "I feel like even that's an understatement. She licked the plate for Celestial's sake."

My brows raise at that, and I walk over and pick up her shiny plate that once homed stir-fry. "I'll get you some more Kindred, there's plenty left," I tell her, squeezing her hand softly and loving her cheeks turning pink under my gaze.

"You don't have to," she remarks, going to stand. "I can get it."

"Nonsense. Let me take care of you, my darling," I say before turning and walking to the kitchen. Nothing in all the worlds is better than providing and caring for my female. I love to make her happy and loved because she deserves it.

CHAPTER TWENTY-ONE

HERMES

The rest of dinner is joyous and filled with happy tales shared around the table from our friends, cracking Havana up at every chance, and I swear I don't think I've ever seen her happier and more at ease. A dark thought tries to flicker in that perhaps she has never been happy until she was here with us, but I brush it away, refusing to let her dark past ruin our future. If she can smile and laugh after everything, then I won't take that from her, not for a second.

"Night guys," Havana choruses to the others as I escort her up the stairwell, my arm wrapped with hers, and her steps light and easy.

I look down at her as we reach her bedroom door and bring her hands to my lips, softly kissing each digit. "I love you," I whisper to her, leaning my head down on hers. "So much."

Havana's little arms reach up and around my neck, dragging

me down to her tiny frame and squeezing me tighter than she ever has. "I love you too, big guy."

My arms encircle her and in this moment I hate the height difference between us because she still feels too far away from me. In the same thought process as me, Havana says, "Pick me up, so I can hold you properly."

Holy shit! Yes!

Without a moment's hesitation, I lift her by her still small waist and Havana wraps her legs around me tightly, bringing her body flush with mine, and I accidentally let out a moan of delight, my hands automatically going to her round ass that fits perfectly in my grasp.

Her body stiffens for just a second before she melts against me, arms snuggling her close and face nuzzled in my bristly neck, where I feel the softest of kisses, and I have to hold back a shudder from the intimate move.

Having Havana's body completely at my mercy like this is the biggest show of trust that she could ever give me, and the weight of that has my eyes burning with tears that threaten to shed. It blows my mind that I can live for so many centuries as a tough warrior, but this small female brings me to my knees and makes me want to weep just from the pure show of her trust.

"Is this okay?" I ask her, just in case.

I feel her smile against my neck, and she answers, "This is perfect. You're not that scary." I love it when she jokes with me.

"I'm a terrifying beast, you know?" I joke back, glad that I can now.

Havana laughs now and leans back to look at me with glittering eyes. Pulling my beard, she crinkles her nose, "Oh yeah. I'm shaking in my boots, buddy." Then she tugs even harder. "What're you gonna do about it?"

"Oh, I'll show you," I rumble out with laughter as I open her door and stalk over to her bed, plopping her down on her butt and immediately start tickling her rib cage.

Letting go of my beard with a squeal, she tries to wriggle back on the bed, but I grab her tiny foot, stopping her. Removing her shoe, I throw it across the room and torture her arch with more tickles as she laughs so hard that she gasps for breath.

"Tell me I'm a scary beast, and I'll let you go," I demand through my own laughter.

"Okay, okay. Mercy," she screams and I stop, waiting for her answer. "I'm a scary beast," Havana giggles out cheekily.

"Oh, you sneaky little thing," I say with fake shock and go back to tickling her foot with enthusiasm. "Say it properly."

Bending over, she grabs her tummy tightly and laughs, but the move reminded me that she was pregnant, and I don't want to upset our baby, so I switch tactics.

"I see how it is," I remark, stopping and lifting her calf to my mouth, looking down at her now still form with a naughty smile. "How do you feel about a lick?" My tongue extends out of my mouth, slowly inching toward her skin.

"No. No. Gross." Havana wiggles, desperate to get free, but my strength is no small feat. "You win. Okay? You win. Stop."

I close my mouth, let go of her leg, and smile wickedly. "Ha ha. Now you know I am the scariest beast of all," I say smugly with a huge grin. "You can't be ruining my image."

Havana sits up and surprises me by climbing into my lap, and I suck in a stunned breath at the move. She snuggles into my chest and plays with a rogue braid hanging over my shoulder. "I'm sorry Hermes, but you will always be my saviour and my hope. You'll never be a beast in my eyes again, so deal with it," she says simply, destroying the last bit of worry I had that she'll leave me.

I put my hand on her cheek and turn her face to mine. "I'm going to kiss you now, darling. Is that okay?" I ask, wanting to make my intentions clear. Even though there is no way, she doesn't feel my rock-hard dick on her ass right now.

With not even a hint of fear, Havana brings her lips to me and kisses me harder than she has before, igniting way too much passion inside me, but I know how to keep pace and not push my luck.

I let her take full control of the kiss and match her when she slides her tongue in my mouth and turns herself to straddle my large frame, her appetite for me veracious and surprising.

I give her everything she wants from me, enjoying the taste and feel of her as she presses herself into me, her hard breasts and small stomach brushing against me. Keeping my hands on her back to not force anything more, I get lost in the moment that seems to simultaneously last forever and is over too soon when she pulls her head back, her full lips red and swollen from our make-out session. It's fucking beautiful.

"Not that I didn't enjoy that because I really, really did, but I didn't think you'd want to do that kind of thing with me," I say, my voice coming out raspier and clearly affected.

Havana touches my lips and looks at them intently with hooded eyes. I'm glad to see she looks as affected as I am. "I wanted to. I- I-," she stutters, looking for the right words and meets my eyes with hers, "I want things I haven't wanted before and don't really know how I feel about it. I just feel," she wiggles in my lap and groans, "things - when I'm close to you, and I don't want to ignore it." Her cheeks flush the deep red colour that I love, and she bites her bottom lip.

"I won't ever deny you because I feel those things too, but I don't want you to rush into anything until you're sure. Okay?" I tell her honestly, my poor cock is hurting from how hard it is right now, but a standing prick has no conscience, and I'm not listening to him right now. "I'm happy to wait forever if you want me to.

Don't do anything just because you think I want it. It's really important that whatever happens between us, you're in control of. It's normal to be nervous because I am too. The last time I was intimate with a female was two centuries ago, so it's not like I'm expecting anything because I'm used to it; but if one day you decide that it's something you want, it's yours to take because I am yours and I will love you in any way that you'll have me."

Havana kisses me softly again, with unshed tears in her eyes. "Thank you." Was all she said as she crawled off my lap with a smile, and I knew it was time for me to leave.

"Good night, little one," I tell her as I walk to the door, turning at the threshold and blowing her a kiss. "If you have a nightmare, just call, and I'll come."

* * *

LEON

"It's time," I smugly tell Twist after receiving the intel from my source in the village near Hermes' territory. "Let's go."

Twist pushes his dread into the back of his armless jacket and lifts the hood, but I don't miss his sneer of distaste at doing my bidding. Unfortunately for him, I own his ass, and he'll do what he's damn well told.

"Yes, sir," he mumbles, beginning to open up the portal that he's good for, and my wicked smile widens at how much fun I'm about to have.

Daddy's coming.

CHAPTER TWENTY-TWO

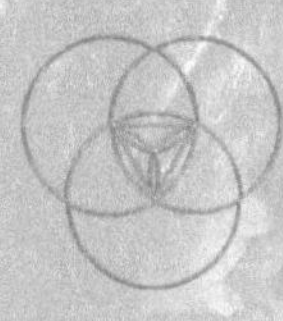

HAVANA

I never get enough of all the floof in this garden. Oh, my God, they're all so cute. Reaching down, I pick up the confident white bunny that adores Hermes and snuggle his fluffy body all over my face.

"I need to give you a name?" I tell him. "I can't believe Hermes never did. How about Thumper? It's a little on the nose, I know, but it just suits you so much."

Thumper's little pink nose twitches, and I take that for a yes.

This garden has become my absolute favourite place to be. Between tending to the vegetables, flowers, and fruit trees and playing with my new little friends, there's nothing better. I have so much more energy lately, now that I'm in my second trimester, and I use every ounce of it, keeping as busy as I can.

I look out to the tree line in the distance, already missing Hermes, even though he's only been gone for two hours. It's the first time he's been away from the property since I've been here, and I really feel his absence.

The other three are here somewhere roaming around, doing their own thing, but it's not the same. My mind trickles to the memory of our passionate kisses last night, and I clench my core tight.

My body has been filled with foreign desires and needs over the last couple of weeks, and it's only growing the more time I spend with Hermes. I wonder if it's a pregnancy thing, but I always heard that women don't like sex when they're knocked up. I can't deny how I'm feeling, though, and it's strong. Never in a million years would I think I'd be so horny over a guy after everything I've been through. It also gives me hope that I can be normal after all.

Hope. What a conundrum that word has become in my life. From the inability to experience its power, to the frantic embrace I have for it now. Because hope is alive and well inside me, its beating heart as strong as mine and bean's. And funny enough, it doesn't even scare me, but instead gives me strength and reminds me that everything's going to be okay from now on.

Before I know what's happening, a bright red light glows no more than five feet from me, that grows into a familiar large circle, but I'm so stunned by what I'm seeing that all I do is stare at it wide-eyed and confused.

To my absolute horror, Leon steps through with one of his favourite generals; his eyes shoot to me instantly, and he smiles wickedly as he steps towards me.

His eyes drop to the small round belly that I have, that's obvious in my too tight shirt, the reason Hermes went to the village today, to get new clothes for me.

"There you are, son," he says cheerily, smirking. "Time to get you home."

No! No! No!

I step backward and then turn to run, screaming as loud as I can, "Help! Help!"

My short legs don't take me far before I'm hoisted from the ground, strong arms wrapping me up so that I can't escape. A terrified scream rips from my throat, and I scratch at the arms covering me, my feet kicking out as wildly as I can. Dread fills me and flashes of memories I can't contain rapidly slam against my brain, but unlike in the past it fires me on, the fear so visceral for not just me, but bean, that I fight. I fight with everything I have, and I scream until my throat feels like it's bleeding.

Leon grins wildly at my outburst as we reach him at the entrance to the portal. "Fight all you like, pet, I love it when they scream."

He chuckles and steps into the portal, and just before I get taken into it, I look back to find the horrified faces of Derryn and Matthew as they run towards us, yelling for me but too late. Much too late.

HERMES

Whistling, I head home with my backpack filled with clothes I had made specially for my love, baby clothes for our son, and a surprise golden ring filled with diamonds that glitter like Havana's eyes when she smiles. I remembered that humans value rings from the males to solidify their union and love. I want to show her how important she is to me, and if a ring will help her understand, then a ring I shall get. *I hope she likes it.*

Sniffing the air, I'm confused when I smell Matthew and... fear? His large white Owl comes into view, flying furiously, swooping down in front of me and shifting before he even hits the ground.

"We've gotta go, brother," he puffs out, sweating and shaking. *What the fuck is happening?* I swear my heart stops when he says the next words. "Leon has her. He came through a portal and took her before we had a chance to get to her. I'm sorry."

Matthew's eyes fill with tears, and I promptly bend over and vomit the entirety of my stomach onto the grass. *She can't be gone.* Ripping my bag off, I throw it at Matthew without a word as fury overflows every one of my senses. *He took my Kindred, my baby.* The clothes I'm wearing tear from my body and I shift, ignoring the pain of such a quick transformation, and turn towards the direction of his village, determined to rip his head from his body with my bare teeth.

A guttural growl rips from me as I plough down every tree in my way. Nothing will stop me from getting my female back, nothing.

Matthew's cries of protest behind me disappear in my haze of rage, my beast fully in control and on the hunt, desperate for blood.

* * *

SUMMER

Putting down my four-and-a-half-month old twins, I marvel again at how much easier they've been than the girls were. Those two refused to ever let me sleep, but Demetrius and Mina are dream babies. Maybe it's a Rathe thing.

Just then, I hear a commotion outside and look out the window to find a man I don't recognise running towards our home, and my interest is instantly piqued.

I walk out the front just as he says to my Reid, "Sir, sir, I'm sorry to burst into your territory like this, but it's an emergency." Reid holds his hands up for him to stop, while Blayze and Salvatore flank him from both sides.

"What's the problem?" Reid asks, not unkindly, but definitely with the authority he's well known for.

The man bends over, looking puffed, and quickly catches his breath. "It's Havana Sir. I have bad news."

Feeling a fire light under my ass, I jog over to them, moving around Reid, and wave him off when he growls at me. "What's wrong with her?" I demand. The stupid man looks behind me. "You better focus right fucking now and tell me what the fuck is going on?"

Clearing his throat nervously, he answers me, as Blayze puts his hand around my waist for support. "Well, um, I just got a message from Twist to bring to Reid as soon as possible."

"Then give my Kindred the damn message already, Craig," Reid growls, sounding as impatient as I feel.

"Sorry. Um, apparently Leon has taken Havana back to his village while she was unsupervised," Craig spit out finally and my heart sinks. "He has her now."

My hand raises to my mouth, and I suck in a breath at the news. "We have to go and help her," I mumble behind my hand. Narrowing my eyes in fury, I drop my hand and stand straight up. "I'll go and get a bag." Turning, I jog back into the house and straight to the bedroom, filling a quick bag with essentials.

"What the fuck's got your knickers in a twist?" Bell asks, plonking herself on my bed unceremoniously.

I explain what's happened as quickly as I can, and her mood gets as serious as mine. "Fuck."

"Yeah. Fuck," I agree. "While I'm gone, I need you to watch the kids. I know it's a lot to ask, but hopefully we won't be gone too long. I have expressed milk in the freezer and plenty of formula if you run out. There's a timetable on the fridge, and it's super easy to follow." I'm not asking, but we both know that. Bell and I are more like sisters than friends now, and things like manners are irrelevant between us in moments like these.

"You owe me. I'll take some Valkyries if you happen to come across any," Bell jokes. "So far I haven't seen even one. Where the fuck are they?"

I laugh at her as I zip up my bag, ready to go. "Firstly, I don't owe you shit. You'll do it because you love them; and secondly, I don't think they come to harmless packs in the forest. I'm sure they've got more important shit to do."

A throat clears behind me, and I turn to see Baine and Reid staring at me and the bag on my back. "Where the hell do you think you're going?" Reid asks with a brow raised.

I tilt my head and scowl at him. "That better be a joke comment. You know exactly where I'm going. I couldn't go last time, and there's no way in fuck I'm sitting this out again, especially now that she's pregnant. You can't actually think I'm going to sit here like a good girl and wait patiently. You know better than that."

"That's exactly what we'd like you to do, lass," Baine admits with a wary sigh. "You cannae be going. You've got bairn to protect."

Bell puts her hand up. "Hi, am I just chopped liver? I'll watch them. Don't worry, they'll be fine. I feed them every two days, right?" she says with amusement.

"That's just wrong." Baine shakes his head and points to her, looking at me. "You cannae be serious?"

I walk to the door, but their two large bodies block the way. "If you don't move, I'm going to remove your balls, and there'll never be little Wolves running around here. Just try me." I squint up at them.

Blayze's laugh comes from behind them. "She's right. Let me in," he says, and they let him pass. He grabs my hand softly, kissing the back of it, and picks me up in a bride hold. "I love your fire, my beautiful Kindred." He sits down on the bed with me on his lap and leans on the bedpost. "Give me some sugar, baby," he tells me, and I can't resist wrapping my arms around him and kissing him hard.

"Ew," Bell groans, "I'm lying on here. Vom."

In a move so quick that I can't track it, Blayze flattens my wrist to the bedpost and some kind of cuff connects me to it. "What the fuck is that?" I ask in shock, and Blayze swiftly slides out from under me and gives my head a quick peck.

"We'll be back as soon as we can," he says and walks out the bedroom door, laughing.

"You son of a bitch," I scream at his retreating form.

Bell, however, thinks it's the best thing she's ever seen in her life and rolls around the bed in a fit of laughter, so I kick the bitch off with a whack. She thuds to the ground and curses. Not so funny now, is it?

I look over to the chuckling Reid with his hands up, slowly backing out of the room. "Love you, baby," he says, blowing me a kiss and disappearing.

How did I get so unlucky to get this bunch of traitors? I think to myself with a huff, pulling on my immovable arm unsuccessfully. "I hate you all!" I yell out.

"Shh, Summer, you'll wake the twins," Salvatore says as he comes in the room, past the nervous looking and silent Baine. I narrow my eyes at the Scottish traitor as Salvatore sits next to me, grabbing my chin and turning my face to his. "Be a good girl, and I might just make it up to you when we get home. How does that sound?" he croons at me and slams his lips on mine, my jaw clenched tightly in his grasp, and I bite his lip hard enough to make it bleed in response.

Being the pain lover that he is, it just gave him a hard on, and he left me there like that with a promise in his eyes of payback, and I see a sore ass in my future.

"I'm sorry, lass," Baine finally says quietly. "I dinnae want you in harm's way. I love you too much."

I sigh and look away at him, secretly happy that I know that at least he'll feel bad about leaving me here like this. Unlike the other barbarians.

Baine gives a key to Bell and tells her to let me free in an hour, before leaving the room with a reluctant glance back at me.

"Undo me," I implore Bell, but the bitch just smiles at me and says, "Sorry, orders are orders. Where was your chocolate stash again? Oh yeah, I remember." I hear her laughing all the way to the kitchen. *Cunt.*

CHAPTER TWENTY-THREE

HAVANA

The red ringed portal closes in front of my eyes, disappearing from view and leaving behind the dreaded image of the familiar locked chamber door in the tower I loathe.

Turning to the side, I watch Twist's crestfallen face at the image of the fear and revelation that's no doubt written all over my face. He looks away from me and mumbles, "Is that everything, Sir?" Leon promptly dismisses him, and Twist can't get out of the room fast enough.

Leon's buff minion turns my body around like I'm a rag doll, so that I'm staring directly into the eyes of my tormentor. The sperm donor sneers at me with satisfaction and waves his hand to the new bed behind him; the steel rings on each corner of the bed is a dead giveaway that any kind of freedom is a thing of the past for me now.

"How do you like the new digs? I made a few modifications since you clearly can't be trusted to run around unsupervised," Leon explains, with excitement brimming in his dark gaze. "And don't worry about Verna, she won't be here to bother you anymore."

The worst-case scenario fills my mind, but I try desperately to brush it away, not willing to accept that he may have killed his own mother. Verna's probably just in another one of Leon's locked rooms.

The brute holding me up, moves me over to the new bed without a word and lays me down, grunting, "Don't move, or I'll knock you out cold. You don't need teeth to birth this baby." Leon laughs heartily at that, while hulk here connects all four of my shaking limbs to the posts of the bed.

I focus on breathing in and out, not letting myself get taken over by my fear, refusing to give him the satisfaction of me checking out again. I need to be strong for Bean, and I'll do whatever it takes to do it.

Leon takes notice of my continued awareness and leans over my face with a dark, twisted smile. "Oh, I see how it is. You wanna play now, do you? Don't get too comfortable, breeder; there's a lot I can do to you that won't hurt my heir." He stands straight back up and points for his general to leave. "I think I'll give you a day to think about what's coming. Twenty-four hours without food and water should grab your attention but not be too damaging to my son."

I harden my eyes at him, refusing to show how scared I am at the idea of Bean not being fed for so long, but I remind myself that I just ate a big meal. We can get through this.

Whistling, Leon casually strolls to the now open door and grabs the handle to close it behind him. Stopping before he does, he tells me with a hint of glee, "Oh, by the way, my Leviathan enjoyed Verna. She was a bit bony but satisfying, nonetheless." He winks and closes the door; the echo of his laugh taunts me as it slowly disappears with his descent.

The tears I shed over the next day, mourning my dear friend Verna, nearly drown me. Grief is a deep pool of despair that never empties; it never goes away. The waters lap at you every moment they can, reminding you of everything you've lost and all your helplessness to change it.

Though I technically didn't know Verna for that long, she became the closest thing I had to a mother since I was a little girl. She gave her life for me to be free and that's more than I deserved, but I will forever be both grateful and regretful because she was worth so much more than the hand she was dealt.

My stomach aches and tightens in hunger, growling loudly at me for not feeding it, and that's the least of my problems. My bladder has given out twice now, and I have to stay lying here in my own filth, my wrists bleeding and sore from my failed attempts to escape. When I call out, nobody comes, and when I cry, nobody cares. Why would they? I'm just an incubator to them, but at least that means I probably won't be raped for a while, especially if I smell like I do now. The putrid stench of my stale urine would even put off an animal. At least, that's the hope.

I watch the slowly darkening window of my tower for the second night in a row, and dread seeps into me. Will Bean be okay for another day without food? I hope so.

Just as I've given up any hope of being fed, the undeniable tread of footsteps on the circular staircase outside my room gets my full attention. Leon pushes the door open, holding a big bowl of food. The smell of grilled fish has my stomach screaming in need.

"I guess that means you're hungry, then?" Leon states sarcastically while he walks over to my side, pulling up a chair that was at the side of the room. "Maybe I'll let you eat it if you say pretty please."

Gritting my teeth, I grind out, "Pretty please." Way too hungry to care about something as insignificant as pride right now.

He laughs at me but moves the fork in the bowl until he pulls it up with a piece of fish and mashed potato on it, and I almost moan at the sight. "Open wide, breeder," Leon says to me like I'm a baby, but I do what I'm told. "So, tell me, did you know about the escape plan or was Verna the mastermind behind it?" he asks conversationally, as if I'm not reeking of piss and shackled to a bed.

"I knew nothing," I answer honestly between chews. "Neither did Verna."

"Interesting." He mulls over my answer and feeds me three more bites before saying, "I truly don't understand the fascination the other faction has with females. Sure, you have tight pussies, but other than that, you don't really have a use. Why on Rathe would a grown ass male risk his life and the life of others just to rescue a pet that they don't even know? It doesn't make sense."

I roll my eyes at his stupidity, and he pulls away the mouthful I was just about to take. "Do that again, and you won't get one more piece," Leon growls in warning. "The only reason I'm feeding you at all is to give my heir strength. If you weren't attached, you'd be dead already."

Getting the hint, I eat the rest of my meal quietly. It's just bland fish and vegetables, but I'll eat anything at this point.

Leon surprises me by putting the dish on the floor, then raising my shirt up to my breasts. I tense straight away; my breathing ceased. "Calm down, I'm not gonna touch you like that. You fucking stink." *Winning*. "I want to see my son's progress. You are, what, just over four months now?" His cold hands press around my stomach, pushing in random places, a questioning look on his face as he tries to work out where Bean is and because I'm so small normally, it's pretty easy to see the little bulge I have now with him in it.

He leans over and shocks me when he starts talking to my belly. At first, I almost think it's sweet until I realise what he's saying. "Don't worry, my little beasty, I'll get you out of this disgusting creature soon, and you won't have to deal with her anymore. Maybe I'll gift you her corpse on your first shift."

"Something's wrong with you, you know that, right?" I mumble under my breath, but he heard me.

"I liked it better when you didn't talk. Go back to that, will you," Leon snaps. "I have a gift for you now that you're fed. Enjoy." He smirks wickedly, and I have a feeling that I'm not going to like this gift one bit.

* * *

LEON

With a twisted satisfaction, I watch Havana's eyes flitter with uncertainty, as her bed head begins to rise until she's upright and facing me directly. *Oh, I'm gonna enjoy this.*

I open the door to her room, where I know three of my best men are waiting. "Go to work," I instruct, and they do, two of them instantly grabbing the mattress behind her and slide it away.

The bigger of the two takes it downstairs, leaving the others to do my bidding, while he replaces the mattress with a clean one. Walking up to Havana, I grab a knife I had in my back pocket and cut open the front of her shirt, bra, skirt and underwear, leaving her bare to our view when they flutter to the ground.

Havana's newfound courage seeps from her as she visibly pales and shrinks in front of me. I grab her clenched jaw in my hand and spit on her face. "It's time you realised your place, breeder. You're nothing but the dirt beneath my shoes, and you'll be treated accordingly. I was way too hospitable before, but not this time."

Raising the power always alive inside me, I call on the ocean and pull a thread of icy water from its depths, into the window of the tower and douse Havana considerably. I enjoy the shrieks of discomfort pouring from her, the frigid temperature a sure shock to a fragile human. Laughing heartily, I continue to soak her from head to toe, loving every second of her naked body trembling, the shaking of her bigger pregnant breasts catches not only my attention but also Virgil's, my head guard.

Virgil holds his hard dick in his hand, thwapping away at the rapturous visual of the little female screaming and shaking, legs wide and open, with water dripping off her sexy curves. My other guard is now gone from the room, taking down the discarded plate from earlier.

I let him finish on the floor in front of him and cut off the stream I produced, returning it to whence it came. Chuckling, I stroll back to Havana and slap her cheek slightly, getting a thrill out of her flinching from my touch. "Much better. Don't you think?"

Her teeth chatter together so loud that it reverberates through the room. The trembling from before is even more violent, if that's possible. I place my hand on her tiny belly and rub it, looking forward to teaching my little Leviathan how to properly torture someone, using his mother as a test dummy.

"It's a shame they didn't care to keep you safer," I comment in ridicule. "It's harder to pick up food than it was to take you. I just strolled right in and out. All done in less than a minute. Pathetic, really, isn't it?" I lean forward and sniff at her. "At least you don't smell like piss or Drake anymore. That's definitely an improvement."

She narrows her eyes at me, and I can't resist poking the bear a little more.

"You do realise that I'm going to kill him for taking my son, don't you? He was a fool to even try it. People fear me for a reason. Perhaps I'll skin his hide and put it in here as a rug to remind you what I do to those that cross me," I add with a laugh. "I'll just leave you here to dry out for an hour or two. I'll get Virgil to bring your mattress replacement later. He seemed to enjoy your company earlier." I nod to the semen he left on the floor. "Especially when you started screaming, and you won't be needing clothes while you're here. Easy access and all that."

She sniffs in a sob and looks up at her wrists, straining in the cuffs, blood trickling down one from holding her weight. "Don't worry, you won't need hands in your job."

I step back and take in her body from top to bottom, stopping at all my favourite parts. My cock hardens in my pants, and I adjust myself. "Maybe, I'll be back in the morning with your breakfast, and get a little something for myself while I'm here."

Leaving her with that thought, I sigh in happiness, actual joy filling me for the first time in ages.

CHAPTER TWENTY-FOUR

HERMES

Like the crazed madman that I am, I run. I run so hard and for so long that I only stop when I can no longer keep going. My beast devours some poor creature and drops to the ground, passing out almost immediately, knowing that I have to be energized enough to take on an entire village by myself. Which I'm one hundred percent ready to do to get my Kindred back.

My slumber is light, and when I hear the snapping of a twig nearby, I jump to my four feet and growl into the surrounding woods at whomever is stupid enough to wake a slumbering beast such as I.

"Hermes, mate. It's just us," Derryn says, coming out of the woods with his hands high. The rest of my friends are behind him, including Sebastian. He must have heard what happened and came to help. "You cannae expect us to bloody stay behind.

Havana's our friend now, and we'll be by your side to take her back."

I let myself relax a bit and shift so that I can speak to them. "Thank you," is all I can say. My rage is still too potent to converse further.

Matthew steps forward. "I brought your weapons and a change of clothes for you. You keep resting, and I'll gather a feast for us to chomp down before we leave. Sebastian, do you mind being lookout? Your senses are excellent."

"Easy done," he agrees easily and nods at me. "I'm so sorry, Hermes. We'll get her back, don't worry." In a flash, he's stripped off his clothes, and his impressive Panther stalks off to check the perimeter.

Knowing better than to disagree with anything that was said because Matthew's right, I shift back into my Drake and almost instantly fall asleep. I will be at my strongest for her, even if it means I have to stop for a while.

* * *

IT'S BEEN THREE DAYS, but we're finally at the same look-out spot we had the first time we came for Havana; but this time is different. This time it's my pregnant Kindred up in that tower, and containing my beast is becoming exponentially more difficult.

There's been no sign of her since we got here, and that makes me even more nervous. I hope to all the Gods she's in there and hasn't been moved to another location.

"What's the plan?" Derryn asks.

"Go through the front door and kill everyone in my way," I answer, and stand up and move down the hill at a fast pace. "Keep up and help, or stay here and watch. Your choice."

"That's nae a plan. That's suicide," Derryn yells, chasing after me as I swing my axes expertly in my grip, getting a good feel of my old friends and undoubtedly getting the attention of the village before me. "Oh feck, we're gonna die. Scooby, try to get to Havana and let her know to be ready. We've got this lot."

Even though the males behind me know how high the risks are following me, they do it anyway. Scooby shifts into his Owl, and the other males brandish their favoured weapons. Derryn's long sword, Sebastian's spear, and Matthew's deadly double daggers. I watch with rising fury as the guards in Leon's village begin to take up arms, preparing for the incoming attack. We may only be five, but we are all skilled warriors and bloodthirsty. The kidnapping of Havana, a heavy hit to all of us but none more than me, and I will have my vengeance.

As I charge forward with my twin axes in hand, three of Leon's guards start charging towards us. I dispose of them with ease, a mere swift movement of my arms. We enter through the gate without any further resistance, the element of surprise on our side.

Heading down the centre of the village, we head directly towards the castle holding my Kindred, the odd passer-by disposed of as they try to intervene.

As we approach the gate of the inner cordon of the castle, Leon's army awaits in front of it, blocking our entrance. Energized by the adrenaline pumping through our veins and the familiar bloodlust our inner warriors crave, we run at them hard, ready to remove their heads from their bodies.

The whistling of arrows rains down around us from overhead; the archers evidently were waiting for this very thing, and it has the five of us swerving in our advance. Unable to secure the safety of the males behind me from the incoming weaponry, I reach inside myself and unleash the power of earth, rising a large barrier from the very ground we're standing on and covering us from the males above.

Derryn, Matthew, and Sebastian join me behind the high mound, with quick thanks as we take guard on both sides, ready for the assault that's sure to come.

Within seconds, the heavy sounds of footfalls approach us, the army ready to counter-attack us in our defensive position, knowing very well that we're sitting ducks, but unfortunately for them, they're going to have to face us.

I look above and see Scooby desperately trying to get headway towards the tower and my Havana, but the barrage of arrows is making it all but impossible. His flying maneuvers are incredible considering the ongoing attack from the archers, and I can't help but to silently commend his bravery.

Ching. Ching. Derryn's long sword and Matthew's swift slicing clash against the incoming guards on the right side, while Sebastian stabs and guts men to my left.

Taking up a position beside Sebastian, I help him to dispose of the constant onslaught of Leon's foot soldiers. One by one we pile the floor at our sides with butchered bodies, my axes always hungry for more.

With the beheading of the next victim, Matthew sucks in a breath and shouts, "Polar Bears. Four of them headed this way."

With a curse, Derryn looks at me. "Time to party," he growls with excitement, stripping off his shirt. "Coming kitty?"

Sebastian gives him the middle finger salute, and they're both shifted into their animals in mere moments.

Knowing that there's no way in hell they can take on one Polar Bear, let alone four, I give my axes a lingering look and put them by Matthew's feet. "Are you gonna be alright?" I ask unnecessarily. We both know he can take all four of us with his eyes closed. His ninja skills are unparalleled. With a smirk and his middle finger, he turns around, continuing to fight the incoming guards.

I crack my neck from side to side and grin as Sebastian's

Panther jumps out from behind the dirt made wall, ripping the closest male apart, Derryn hot on his heels. I let my beast take over, careful not to crush the wall I made earlier with my colossal size so that Matthew can keep using it.

Instantly, Leon's soldiers freeze in their approach and look up with fear in their eyes. *That's right, fuckers, you should be afraid.* Stomping down on the closest male, his body disintegrates into a gooey mess of blood and bones under my weight.

Out of the corner of my eye, I see white fur barreling towards my shifted friends and move to intervene, successfully cutting them off. Unfortunately, that's the same time a ballista arrow slices along the side of my neck, raising a roar out of me. Looking up, I'm surprised to see eight ballistae being loaded and aimed directly at me.

I swipe one angry Polar Bear away that tries and fails miserably to take a chunk out of my front leg. My armoured scales are much too strong for their measly teeth.

Two more ballista arrows smash against the scales on my back. While they can't pierce the stronger scales of my back, it still hurts like a bitch and almost has me buckling over from the intense pain. *Fuck.*

Trying to ignore the agony on my back and scratching of the Polar Bears, I continuously bat them away from where Derryn and Sebastian are fighting hard to take down as many guards as they can while dodging the incoming arrows from the archers above.

Matthew cries out, and I swing my large head in his direction, lifting a piece of ground into a spear and slicing through the male that had just stabbed him in the back. He waves in thanks, showing me he's still good to fight, and I focus back on the Polar Bear in front of me, trying to scratch at my weaker belly scales.

Bending, I rip his head clean off his body with my sharp,

curved teeth like he's made of butter, spitting it back out at his friend roaring at me nearby.

I lift my head up and a ballista arrow flies past my neck, missing it by just inches. My back, legs, top of head, and tail are covered with impenetrable armoured scales, but my neck, eyes, chest, and belly are my weak spots. Weak enough that a ballista arrow could definitely slice through it, ending me.

Another four arrows rain down on me one after the other, aiming for my weaker scales. Several of them almost reach their targets and cause me considerable pain.

Sebastian's Panther growls in pain, and I turn to find his back sliced by one of the Polar Bears that must have slid by when I was defending myself against the arrows. Derryn nips and circles the Bear, dancing around him to keep out of his flailing grasps.

With a weary jog, I twist my head as I reach them, impaling the beast with my left horn. His lifeless body twitches and hangs from the tip. The sight is both gruesome and victorious. I fling his body to the side with a quick shake and check on my friend.

The Panther mewls in pain, his back wound open and bleeding profusely. Derryn's Wolf stands over him, growling at the incoming guards stabbing at them both while they're clearly tired and weak.

Matthew, seeing what's happened to Sebastian, comes running over, slicing up bastards as he runs, his technique with the curved, double daggers something to behold.

"We need to push back a bit," Matthew cries out as he reaches us, panting heavily. "More males just came running out of the castle door. There's no way we can keep progressing with Sebastian in this condition, and I haven't seen Scooby for a few minutes now. I have no idea if he made it inside or not, but it can't hurt to recoup."

Nodding reluctantly, I turn to face the incoming foot soldiers and attack them several at a time while Derryn and Sebastian shift back. A cry of pain from the male in question letting me know he was successful.

I fight them all off single-handed, while being hit with four more ballista arrows, until I hear Matthew tell me to move.

Backing up, we slowly get out of there, Matthew and Derryn practically carrying the injured Sebastian. We manage to make it to the outer gates, all the while having to defend from the land and air.

When we step outside the large archway, heavy iron gates close, effectively denying us reentry to the grounds. Furious at the outcome, and devastated that I couldn't reach Havana, I roar my agony into the air.

Just when I think it can't get any worse, pained screams tear from the tower. Female screams. My Havana's screams. Over and over again, and I almost topple over from the sound alone.

What's he doing to her?

The screaming stops suddenly, and Leon's loud, joyous laughter rings clear. And everything around me turns red.

CHAPTER TWENTY-FIVE

HAVANA

Shouts and clanking wake me from a restless slumber, my body cold and exposed, but at least I'm in the horizontal position again. My poor wrists aching terribly from alternating between being upright and lying down.

"Soothing isn't it?" Leon's voice says from the back of the room, scaring the shit out of me.

I yelp in surprise, my heart pounding in my chest like a little drum. He has a knack of popping up when I least expect it, but it's mostly just to mess with me, I think. So far, he hasn't really hurt me or taken advantage of me sexually. He's focused on degrading me more than anything, which is a type of torture in itself.

Random growls join the sounds of a battle below, and a little piece of my heart whispers, *Maybe?* Hope. The thing I refuse to ever give up again. Yes, it's scary and painful sometimes, but I need fuel to feed my soul, to remind me why I need to keep fighting for Bean.

"Don't look too excited, pet," Leon snickers. "They're extremely outnumbered, and we're ready for them this time. They'll be dead within the hour. I guarantee it."

I just sneer at him, choosing to be quiet so I don't distract Hermes and the others. I refuse to put fuel on an already heated fire. Closing my eyes, I turn my head away and focus on what I can hear.

A pained roar comes from what I assume is Hermes, and I hold my breath, choosing to believe that he's okay because he has to be. We need him to be. More noises continue, and that's enough of a confirmation for me to know he's alright. The men screaming down there must be Hermes' victims as he fights to get to me, and a small smile lines my lips.

Leon slams his hand down next to my head, and I flinch at the sudden violence, my eyes snapping open. His close vicinity to my face has bile rising in my stomach. The very idea of him this close to me is enough to make me sick.

"I never said that you were allowed to smile, did I?" he growls at me, displeased by my moment of defiance.

I meet his eyes dead on because I'm not the girl that I used to be, and I never will be again. One of his brows lifts in surprise, but I don't move or say a word, just stare him down. Just because I'm below him right now doesn't mean that I'm beneath him, and I let my eyes show that loud and clear.

Frantic fluttering gets both of our attention, and we both turn our heads to see Scooby's Owl clumsily land inside my window, an arrow straight through his left wing.

With swift movements, Leon bounds over and grabs Scooby's Owl by the neck and wraps a rope around it that he pulls out of his back pocket. It's on so tight that it's clear to see that he can barely breathe.

"You can't shift now, can you, birdie?" Leon mocks, holding him by both of his large wings. "Unless you feel like being decapitated today?"

"Stop it Leon," I plead. "Let him go. I'll do whatever you want, just please let Scooby go."

Leon scowls deeply at me. "This is exactly what I'm talking about. Why would you think I want you to do anything for me in exchange for this idiot's life? I own you, and you will do whatever I say, regardless. In fact," he looks down at the Owl trying to scratch at him with his claws, with a little too much eagerness for my liking. "How about I show you how little I give a fuck?"

He shoves Scooby's struggling form down on the floor, beak first, and pushes him flat with his foot. Scooby screeches out in pain, but in a quick motion, Leon rips both of his wings straight from his body in one tearing motion.

Blood sprays everywhere, and Leon pushes down harder with his foot at the same time, crushing his head under his boot. Scooby's remaining body, limp and lifeless. A bloody mess that I'll never forget.

Turning my head, I vomit on the bed beside me. The sight is too much for me to deal with. The memory of this will haunt my nightmares for the rest of my life. My friend is now dead, and in the most horrific way possible. Leon really is a monster.

"What's wrong, pet? The truth too hard to swallow?" Leon chuckles out, completely unfazed by what he just did to my friend.

Tears pour from my closed eyes. I tell myself that I need to be strong, but I'm not sure if I can be *this* strong. Can anybody?

"You don't have to be too scared, you know? I'm not going to kill you. Yet." Leon's words are no solace to my pain.

I focus on my breathing and nothing else, determined not to slip into another one of my dazes, but Leon's quiet growl gets my attention. I look over to him, purposely not looking at the floor, or more specifically, what's on it. Leon's leaning out of the window glaring down at the scene below, not happy with the progress, apparently.

A feline growl gives me goosebumps, the poor creature sounding like it's in terrible pain, and I watch as Leon's features start to slowly change into one of satisfaction, and he swivels his head to look between me and the battle below. An idea formed before me. An idea I'm surely going to hate.

"Maybe you will come in handy after all, and I get to have a bit of fun at the same time." Leon stalks over to me, removing the knife from his back pocket that he always seems to have on him. "Seems they retreated out of the village. I can't have that now, can I? Time to sing, pet."

Not knowing what the hell he's talking about, I narrow my eyes at his purely evil smile, but I find out what he means almost immediately when he slides his knife across the top of my thigh.

Unable to keep it in, I scream as he slices the deep gash into me. One thigh and then the other, before bringing it to my collarbone and slicing me open from my left side to my right like a grim smile, dripping in blood. I scream and scream, the pain intense and hard to deal with.

"That's it, pet, sing for me." Leon laughs out loud. "Scream just the way I like it."

He stabs hard down on the side of my thigh, and the pain takes me deep into darkness, where it can't hurt me anymore. The last thing I remember is Leon's hysterical laughter and maybe... fire?

CHAPTER TWENTY-SIX

HERMES

A flash of red and unbelievable heat soars over the top of us, and I stare in awe at what is the spectacle of Blayze in his Phoenix form. The sight of his majestic beast stuns me, as it's done every time I've seen it, and it's no wonder that the legend of the Phoenix pulls fear from even the most courageous of males.

The long feathered flames lick across Leon's village, reaping havoc with every touch. Sides of buildings all but disintegrate under the intense heat that only a Phoenix can bring.

An earth-shattering roar bellows from above me as a gargantuan shadow blocks out the sun; the might of Salvatore's red and black Dragon joins his Kindred brother in the destruction. His fire streams from his great jaws, strafing in the opposite path, crossing his own fire with Blayze's blistering one.

The obliteration before me comes as such a surprise that I'm momentarily captivated by the scene. That is, until the alpha's howl rises from the hill behind us, followed by a chorus of answering war cries from what could easily be a hundred Wolves.

I turn to see Derryn shift into his own Wolf, joining in on the undeniable order to prepare for battle. His stance takes up a protective position; his legs bracketing our injured friend underneath him, showing that he will fight any that dare come near.

Matthew turns to me with a kilowatt smile and says, "They're here for you, brother, like you have always been there for them." Hitting his chest with his fist, he bows slightly to me. "It's been an honour to fight with you."

I place my hand on his shoulder and look up towards the now silent tower and answer quietly, "They're here for that innocent female, and I will forever be grateful to them and to you. I owe each of you a debt." I nod to all three of my friends, my worry for Scooby's whereabouts growing.

Reid's giant black Wolf sprints down the hill towards us, Baine's red Wolf right behind him. The myriad of shifters following their stead blows my mind; Wolves, Grizzlies, Cheetahs, and even Neville and a few of his Siren friends.

"Time to focus, Hermes," Matthew tells me in a strained voice, looking at the village behind me. "We've got company."

Turning to see what he's talking about, the gate of the village lifts back up and a fuck load of guards come pouring out, armed to the teeth and ready for more.

Reid stops next to us and shifts. As his army continues on to the approaching guards, he asks without preamble, "Where is she?"

"In the top of the tower." I point over, and to my horror, the flames from below are starting to rise up the side of the tower, decimating it one tenth at a time. "We need to get to her." Panic rides me hard.

Baine's Wolf nips at his brother playfully, obviously happy to see him after such a long absence, and Derryn allows it, even though he's on guard.

"Hermes. I get that you want to get to Havana, I really do, but right now you're needed in the fight. I can get in and out a lot faster than you can, and no one will be watching me as closely as they'll be watching you," Reid tells me, authority in his voice. "Let me get your Kindred for you. You go and get that son of a bitch that did this to her."

Well, if he's going to put it like that. "I'm trusting you," I grumble, an unsaid threat in my voice, and he nods his understanding.

I shift back into my Drake form and look at Matthew.

"Derryn and I will stay here and guard Sebastian," Matthew says, "You go ahead. Go fuck him up, brother."

Reid shifts and takes off with Baine into the flurry of battle between factions. One of so very many. When will the bloodshed end? With a deep breath, I focus my attention on the open gate, intent on plowing past anyone in my way until I reach my intended target.

Bodies of my enemies drop around me like flies, bathing my brown scales in blood. My large clawed feet squish their remains between my toes, but I don't stop. Nothing can make me stop now. My faction does everything they can to exterminate the others with extreme prejudice, freeing my need for any unnecessary battle on the way.

I run through the centre of the village again, but unlike before, it's now alight with flames, Salvatore and Blayze randomly selecting places below them to ignite. I don't let the heat slow me down, barreling through with renewed vigour. Victory, surely on the horizon.

The inner wall before the castle has partially crumbled, and I easily make my way over it, using my earth power to part the debris as I go.

A humongous Polar Bear stands on his back legs in front of the door, a sentinel for the building and meant to instil fear. Unfortunately for him, he is nothing more than a fly for me to swat out of the way.

Surprising me, the Bear shifts into his humanoid self and smiles at me with the look of a man who's already won. "You must be the overgrown lizard?" he yells at me as I approach. "I'm Virgil, and I just wanted to say thank you."

His words have me stopping in my tracks in front of him. I look down at his small form below my own and turn my head to the side in question. *Thank me? What for?*

"Your female," Virgil starts. "Watching her naked and screaming for mercy. Mmm, mmm. I've never jizzed so hard in my life." He grabs his crotch and shakes it at me.

I narrow my eyes, and with merely a thought, send a spike of sharp stone straight up from the ground, cutting off his cock and balls. The second spike, however, shoves right up his ass, lifting the fucker off the ground. Virgil suspends helplessly as his own body weight slowly pushes him further down the bloody skewer.

Leaving him to his fate and reveling in Virgil's gurgled screams, I step around him, but before I go to break down the front wall of the castle to gain entry, I notice movement in my periphery. Whipping my head to the side, I catch Leon stepping out the side door beside the cliff face and change direction immediately.

With a low growl, I caught his attention. My lips curl up in anger, showing the full row of my sharp, curved teeth. Spittle drips from my mouth as the hunger to taste his blood becomes visceral.

"Good. You saved me the trip." Was all Leon said before ripping through his clothes. His ocean coloured serpentine

Leviathan tears forth, and we bolt towards each other with a bloodlust that won't be denied.

* * *

LEON

Whack.

My tail flings out, smashing Hermes' ugly ass Drake right in the face, pushing him back a few steps. Before he has time to retaliate, I follow it up with a heavy blast of icy water into his open jaws, effectively choking him with the sea.

I've been wanting to fuck up this righteous prick for a century. He may be older than me, but I refuse to believe that his sad excuse for a Dragon could ever match my Leviathan.

The Drakes spiked tail swooshes towards me, but I manage to avoid it easily with my lithe body. A spike of stone slices my back suddenly, and I realise the tail was a diversion. The pain rips through me, but luckily no vital organs were punctured.

Rocks start to rain down on me from every direction, and I use the speed of my tail to deflect a lot of them. A few hard hits got through, leaving me in even more pain; the scent of my blood wafts through the air, and I know I have to get the upper hand now that the first blood is shed.

At top speed, I slither my body around the great mass of Hermes' Drake, my tail wrapping around his thick throat and squeezing as hard as I can. My jagged teeth rip into his side, the scales there slightly softer than his back.

Hermes surprises me by pushing himself over, landing on his back with me still encircling him. His sharp spikes pierce me in several places, but I bite him again, ripping in deeper, stifling any sounds of pain.

Rolling back and forth, Hermes' mass begins to crush me and, in an effort to push him off, I pull a large sphere of seawater over, covering his head with it in an attempt to drown him. It works, and his large claws try to grab at his neck, desperate for the air that's never coming, if I get a say in it.

I remove myself carefully from Hermes' flailing form and smirk down at him in an offensive position, ready to use my talons to rip his head off. A shriek of pain rips from me, as a long stone spear drives through my back, protruding from my chest. Blood bubbles from my mouth, and in a momentary lapse of control, the water surrounding Hermes splashes to the ground.

With quick movements, I rip the spear out of my chest, wrap myself around Hermes' neck and fling his heavy head into the cliff's edge with a fury. The cracking of his skull is an audible snap.

With victory, I give a toothy grin down at my almost unconscious unworthy foe, grab his leg with my tail, and fling Hermes into the raging sea below. I dive after him, energized and excited to finish him in my element.

Nobody can best me in the sea, and certainly not an already half-dead stone lizard.

CHAPTER TWENTY-SEVEN

HAVANA

"Holy fuck," I hear in the back of my mind, pain splitting through me from everywhere. "Havana? Female, please answer me."

Reid?

Someone's touching my feet. *What's happening? Why am I hurting so much?* I screech in pain when I try to move my leg.

"Shhh, it's alright. It's Reid. I'm getting you out of here." His voice hitches, which confuses me almost as much as the pain, and I open my eyes when I feel him touch my cheek softly. "I'm so sorry."

The light in the room has me squinting, but when my eyes focus, I'm stunned to see a tear on Reid's cheek, his eyes glassy. *What's wrong?*

Then it all comes back to me, in a horrific reel of blood and pain. I let out a sob, and Reid's face flinches like I hit him.

Looking down at my screaming body, I take in the mess of me, now lying down again. Blood, new and old, cakes my wounds, and I'm still as naked as I remember, but at least my legs are closed now that they're not tied up anymore.

Reid quickly moves to my aching wrists and rips the shackles off me like they're nothing, rendering a scream from me. The raw skin ripped open and mutilated.

I sniff and am surprised when all I can smell is smoke. Seeming to read my thoughts, Reid says quickly, "I know you're hurting, but we've got to go. The entire village is on fire, and we don't want to get stuck up here; I don't know about you, but I don't have wings."

Wings... Scooby.

Another sob rips from me, and I slowly sit up, turning my face to the heart-wrenching sight of my friend, a crumpled mess.

"Shit," Reid curses, carefully taking my legs off the table so I can stand. "Terrible use of words. Please forgive me." The pain in Reid's eyes, and the way he doesn't look at Scooby, tells me that he was his friend as well.

Reid rubs his face, looking at the door. The whole time he was helping me, I noticed that he took great pains to give me as much dignity as he could, under the circumstances. He only looked at my face and hands, but I'm sure there's no way to truly block out how terrible I look.

I touch my belly and hope that Bean is okay. Slowly, I lower myself to the ground. "Let's go," I croak, my throat sore from screaming earlier.

"Here." Reid takes his shirt off and passes it to me, still looking away. "I had one of the others carry my clothes because I didn't want to frighten you. I changed before climbing the stairs. I didn't think that you... I didn't think. I'm sorry."

"Please stop apologising," I murmur, taking his shirt and cringing as Reid helps to put it on. My body hurts so much, but I don't want to burn to death, so I suck it up and move as quickly as I can.

Blood quickly starts coating the shirt from my various wounds, but I don't care. At least it's long enough to cover all the essentials.

I hobble over to him. "Thank you," I say, truly meaning it. Reid has only ever been kind to me.

Reid looks at me with an odd expression, "I think this is the most I've ever heard you say."

"I'm different now," is all I say, limping out the door.

Reid follows behind me and mumbles, "I can see that."

The smoke gets thicker as we reach the bottom of the stairwell, as it flows in from the open door. Reid grabs some way-to-big shoes from the doorway for me and helps me slip them on so that I don't burn my feet. We hold our breath and walk through the door, my eyes burning from the smoke and heat all around. I stay as close to Reid's side as I can, and at one point, the visibility becomes so bad that I happily take his hand and let him lead me through until we reach a clearing.

Reid stops short, turning his head at the cliff beside the castle. There's not as much smoke over there, but what does catch my attention makes my heart stop.

"We have to get Hermes," I frantically tell Reid, as we watch the battle before us unfold. *I can't leave without him.*

Leon's Leviathan is nothing like I imagined. His long body is more the Chinese version of a dragon, but his head is long and angular like a butch snake; his jagged teeth protrude through his lips, long and angular. While Hermes' Drake battles on all four legs like a two horned, scaled triceratops with large taloned claws instead of stumps, and deadly spikes over his tail and parts of his lower back, the Leviathan stands up on his back legs, using his snake-like body to constrict and dodge, while his front legs are more like clawed hands, grabbing and scratching.

The sight is absolutely terrifying as they tear each other apart bit by bit, and the worst part is that Leon seems to be winning as he chokes the life from the man I love.

Hermes rolls, trying to get him off, but Leon attacks his side, blood pouring from the wound. Rolling more, it looks as though Hermes might be starting to crush him, Leon's beast crying out.

"We need to go to safety, female," Reid pleads, pulling on my elbow, but I rip it back from him, determined not to leave Hermes.

A weird ball of water covers Hermes as Leon slivers free, but almost as soon as he does, a spear of stones comes from somewhere and skewers Leon through the chest.

I almost cry out in glee, but before I get a chance to, time slows down as Leon does some freakish manoeuvre, slamming Hermes' head into the ground. The crack echoes over the distance, and with it, my soul cracks, too.

He doesn't move. *Why won't Hermes get up?* "Oh, my God," I whisper, my hand going to my throat in horror. "Hermes?"

With a fling of his tail, Leon flings Hermes over the cliff and into the depths of the ocean, and follows after him.

All I can hear as I run-hobble to the cliff edge is my own scream.

* * *

HERMES

Freezing cold water swallows me with what sounded like Havana's screams. I try with a desperation I've never known to stay awake as darkness threatens to take me. My head pulses with extreme agony, my skull no doubt broken.

I feel myself sinking lower and lower into the sea, my body heavy and cumbersome in the water, and I'm unable to swim in this form, which Leon assuredly knows, and that's why he threw me in here instead of continuing to fight me on land.

I have almost zero chance of survival now, but that doesn't mean I'm going to give up easily. I don't care what I have to do, but if I'm going to hell, then Leon's coming with me.

My lungs start to burn for air, fighting my head for top pain, and I let myself shift down to a man, hoping that Leon doesn't just eat me with one gulp.

I flail around in the depths, trying to figure out which way is up, when the Leviathan swims by my now frail form, knocking me as he goes, playing with his prey.

Blackness flickers over my vision from both my head injury and my lack of oxygen, and Leon nudges me again. *Which way is up, damn it?*

Swimming with all my might, I just pick a direction and hope for the best. Trying to see under water is hard, but a wall of rock appears before me and I aim for it, unsure if it's actually a wall or the bottom of the ocean, but at least it's a destination.

I reach my hands out and pat at the surface with relief, turning around just in time to see Leon swimming straight for me. I flatten my hand on the wall behind me and his taloned hand swipes at me with precision, ripping me open from my belly button to my chest at the same time I send a thin, wide, razor-sharp, guillotine blade of my own making rips from the wall behind me, decapitating him instantly.

The water around me turns red with the blood we both lose, and my last thoughts are of the beautiful female that owns me, heart, body, and soul. I would gladly die for her again and again if it meant she would be free and safe. I only wish I could have seen our son, just once.

Painfully breathing in my last breath of water, I let go, with her big brown eyes and full smile taking me home.

CHAPTER TWENTY-EIGHT

HAVANA

"Nooo!" I scream and scream, with no sign of either Dragon. No splashing, no bobbing, no anything. Just waves and waves of uninterrupted sea.

Reid grabs my arm, trying to pull me away from the edge. "Step back, Havana. You have to think of the baby. Hermes wouldn't want you two dying trying to get to him," he tells me, getting through my fearful melt down.

I get down on the floor carefully and let just my head lean over, making sure not to put myself and Bean at risk because Reid is absolutely right.

With a heavy sigh of resignation, Reid sits close beside me, leaning down to see what I see. Still nothing.

"How long can they hold their breath?" I ask.

"Leon can forever, he has gills, but Hermes will have to come up for air sometime. Mhanu are sturdier than humans, he can hold his breath for longer than you would be able to but not by much," Reid tells me honestly.

We watch and we wait, but nothing happens. Eventually we're joined by Salvatore and Blayze, both sitting beside us without a word. They must have seen what happened from the air.

I turn to them and ask with narrowed eyes, "Why didn't you help him?" The accusation in my voice is clear, but I don't care.

"This was his battle to fight Havana. I know you don't understand that, but it was his right as your Kindred to fight on your behalf and for us to interfere would be dishonourable for him, and Hermes is one of the most honourable men I know. I wouldn't take this from him. Give him time, he might just surprise you."

Unfortunately, the moment he said that, the sea below us changed. All along the cliff below, the waves crashed in deep red clouds, bubbles of it floating to the surface, and I clutch at my chest, praying to any God that will listen for that to be Leon's blood.

A hand squeezes my shoulder on one side, and from the other side a heavy arm wraps around me. Looking over, I see Salvatore holding me close, his eyes deeply sombre and swimming with regret.

I shake my head from side to side like a madwoman and look back down into the tumultuous surf. *No. No. No.* I squint, needing to see through the water, needing to know what's happening, and Leon's grotesque head bobs to the surface, clearly separated from his body.

I look up at Salvatore hopefully, but he just looks at Reid behind me with sad eyes.

"Look," I practically yell, my throat hurting from the effort. "It's Leon that died. Why do you keep looking like that?"

Salvatore huffs out a breath and looks me straight in the eyes as he breaks my heart. "Female, we can scent that blood, and it's just as much Hermes' as it is Leon's. I'm so sorry, but that's too much blood."

What? But his head...

I can't comprehend what he's telling me, and I look back down, cringing at the disgusting sight of Leon's head, his eyes still open.

"We need to go now and get you warmed up," Blayze says, holding his hand out with a flame in the centre, trying to keep me warm, I suppose, but I don't want to go. I can't go without Hermes.

"He'll be okay," I choke out. "He has to be." My voice gets smaller and smaller as I talk, my hope tired but refusing to give up the fight for happiness.

I cover my face with my hands and try not to sob, because if I start, I don't think I'll ever stop.

"What the fuck?" Reid says, startling me. "Salvatore, get down there."

Looking back down, I gasp at a naked man face down, bobbing in the water below, blood soaking into surrounding waves. *Hermes!* I'd know those braids anywhere.

In a flash, Salvatore shifts and flies down, carefully plucking Hermes from the waters with this humongous claw and flying up to where we wait, my hands wringing together. All the pain in my body is forgotten, and my entire focus is on whether or not Hermes is breathing.

With expert movements, Salvatore places his body onto the bench sitting nearby, and I run to him, stopping before I reach him, my hand covering my mouth in horror.

Hermes' body is sliced open up the middle, and the sight has me falling to my knees and retching. Salvatore shifts back and starts working on Hermes' body, desperately trying to get him to breathe. Blayze joins in, working on pushing breath into his mouth while Salvatore massages his half open chest, pushing down on it so hard that I can't watch. Reid kneels silently beside me, comforting me with his presence, but nothing is going to make me whole again unless the man before me wakes up and calls me little one or darling.

I can't lose him; I just can't.

Hearing people running, I look over to see Matthew and the Sorcerer that kept taking me away. As they reach us, I pick up the closest stone and throw it at Twist, hitting him in the head, and he reels back and looks down at me, his face changing from shock to guilt in seconds. *Yeah, you should feel guilty.*

"Havana," Matthew says beside him, reading the fury and despair on my face. "He's here to help."

"He did this," I sob. "None of this would have happened if he'd just left me alone."

Twist's hood falls back from the ocean breeze, and there's no mistaking the regret written all over his face, but he remains silent, not coming to his own defence or giving me any excuses. He just stands there and accepts my words for the reality they are.

"I know and so does he, believe me, but he's come to help if you'll let him," Matthew explains patiently, his hand pointing in Hermes' direction. "Let him help."

I nod once but stare Twist down, unwilling to take my eyes off him for a second in case he hurts Hermes instead.

Twist rubs his fingers together and little sparks of magenta flicker from them. Walking over to Hermes, he nods to Salvatore and Blayze and they both stop what they're doing, stepping back and letting Twist take over. His now magenta fingertips touch Hermes' chest, and his body twitches up like he was electrocuted. The sight reminding me of a defibrillator. He does it two more times before sighing in relief and stepping back.

Blayze tips Hermes to his side as water pours from his lips, and he coughs violently.

I'm so shocked that he's moving that I just sit there, staring.

Hermes' body gets put back down, and Blayze looks at Reid and nods to me.

Reid grabs my face and turns it away from Hermes. I struggle in his hold, but he's so strong that it makes no difference whatsoever. Letting me go he apologises, but I narrow my eyes at him about to argue when I look at Hermes and notice that his wounds, while still gruesome, are closed in the worst affected areas, his organs no longer on display for all to see.

"What happened?" I ask in awe, confused by the sudden change.

"He's stable for now," Salvatore says, obviously relieved. "It's time to get you and him to safety and away from any potential threats."

I notice that he didn't answer my question, and I'm presuming he's not going to either. I figure I can ask later when things have calmed down, and I focus on what to do right now.

"There's one guard that seems worse than the others. Virgil. Has anyone seen him?" I ask, and don't miss the smirk on Matthew's face. "What?" I ask him.

"Let's just say that I saw him on my way, and you don't need to worry about Virgil anymore," Matthew answers. "I'd put money on Hermes reaching him before he got to Leon." I frown at him, wondering how he knows that, but he just shakes his head. "Trust me, you don't want to know."

Taking his word for it, I let the subject drop and watch as Salvatore and Blayze carefully lift Hermes' injured body and look at Twist. "You gonna help with this?" Blayze asks him. "It's the least you can do."

"There will never be enough that I can do," Twist says, opening the portal that I've grown to loathe more than anything.

Matthew and Reid help me back to my feet, and my pain

comes back in twofold. Crying out, my body sags, and they basically carry me through the portal after Hermes.

"You look terrible," Matthew says quietly, as we come through to the front door of our house.

"Thanks," I grumble, and he chuckles.

Matthew leans his head on mine. "Better terrible than dead, female." And truer words couldn't be spoken.

They move us both into the lounge and place us down on opposite couches, covering our battered and sliced bodies with blankets from nearby. All the while, I never take my eyes off Hermes' unconscious face.

I'll never take a moment of us together for granted ever again. Now, I just need him to wake up, so I can tell him how much I love him.

A flutter inside my stomach surprises me, and I place my hand over my small bump. *Is that you, Bean?* I ask my baby in my head, and he answers with another soft flutter, and I know everything's going to be okay.

CHAPTER TWENTY-NINE

HAVANA

For three months, Hermes sleeps.

Healers come and go at my request, but none of them ever seem concerned. Something about his body being healed but his mind needing rest. His head injury was by far the worst of his injuries, and if we hadn't gotten to Hermes as quickly as we did, there's no doubt that he wouldn't have made it.

I sent Matthew again yesterday to fetch the local healer. I don't care for their blasé attitude toward Hermes' recuperation. Dr Orion was the only one that seemed to be truly honest with me, telling me that there's a chance that Hermes will never wake up because he could have permanent brain damage. But once again, the only thing that I was told to do was wait. How long am I supposed to wait, though?

Since that fateful day, neither Matthew nor I were ever the same again. While I became a confident mother hen, ordering everyone about like the house matriarch, poor Matthew has become more and more recluse. The once vibrant man, a shell of his former self after losing his best friend, Scooby.

I'll never forget the moment that Reid told Matthew how he found Scooby, and when Matthew searched me out later that day for details, I couldn't bring myself to speak to them. All I could give him was an apology and a promise that he didn't want to know. I know this because I wish I didn't know.

Every night my sleep is plagued with horrific scenes of Scooby's final moments or Hermes' body falling off into oblivion. I still have the odd ones from my past or either time I spent with Leon, but they seem to have taken a backseat for now. The majority of my midnight screams are for the loss of others instead of my own demons.

I stare down at Hermes' still form in his gargantuan bed and reach over for his hand, lifting it to my mouth and kissing each knuckle with reverence. I miss him talking to me, or even just looking at me. I miss him.

"Time to wake up, big fella," I whisper over the skin on his palm, his big hand heavy in my small ones. "I need you. We need you." I stand and place his palm on my now large and distended stomach.

I can only pray at this point that he'll wake up in time to be here when our son is born because I don't think I can get through labour without him. Reid offered to take us both back to his pack until Hermes wakes up, but I want him to be in our home when he comes to.

Derryn and Sebastian didn't come back with us because I was technically not under immediate threat anymore. Plus, Sebastian needed to go off to heal his own wounds, while Derryn was called away for work. Apparently, there was some kind of issue with the

Stag shifters because of a female causing shit, and he had to go sort it out.

Different people have popped in to see us over time, checking up on how we're doing, and have offered again and again, but I refuse to budge. My mind made up. Now that my due date is looming closer, I'm wondering if I should see if one of them is willing to come and stay with me for a little while. I'm glad that I have Matthew, but he's in no shape to help me at the moment because he can barely help himself.

Focusing on the daily routine that keeps me sane and my brain busy with chores, I get up and gather a clean towel, flannel, and basin, ready to give Hermes a sponge bath. I've become a lot better at it over time, but my stomach can really get in the way these days. I do his front in the mornings, and Matthew flips him over for me in the afternoons so that I can do his back.

Amazingly, Hermes doesn't need an IV or catheter because of some kind of magic that I honestly still don't understand. His large body never seems to deflate or change in any way; he's just in some kind of 'sleeping beauty' state.

Hermes has to have a Sorcerer come weekly to perform the spell over him to keep it activated. It's usually very expensive, apparently because it uses a humongous amount of magic and is exhausting for the person performing it. However, Twist has taken it upon himself to do it as some kind of penance, and I'm certainly not going to turn it down, even though his presence still makes me understandably nervous.

A knock sounds at Hermes' bedroom door, and Matthew sticks his head in with a wan smile. Instantly, I'm taken aback again by how pale he is; the dark bags under his eyes reminding me that I'm not the only one not sleeping.

"Doc's here," Matthew says flatly.

Putting down my haul from the bathroom at the end of the

bed, glad that I haven't put the water in it yet, I reply, "Bring him in."

"How's the patient today?" Duff, the local Sorcerer and healer, asks me with a soft voice and kind eyes. "Any change?"

I brush my hands down the front of my dress and answer, feeling frustrated, even though I know it's not Duff's fault. "Obviously not, or I wouldn't have called you back again."

Duff walks over to Hermes and checks his vitals without another word. When he's done, he takes a seat in the chair beside Hermes, turning his body to face me and crossing his legs with his hands in his lap. "Havana, I don't know what you're asking me to do here," Duff states quietly.

"I want you to wake him up. Fix him. Something." My voice comes out more hysterical than I mean it to.

Duff sighs and leans forward in the chair. "Why don't I look you over while I'm here?" He completely ignores my pleas for Hermes.

"Do *not* patronise me. I'm fine. All I have is scars and a baby. Hermes is the one that needs you." I know logically that Duff is doing the best he can, but the longer Hermes sleeps, the more scared I am that he won't wake up again.

"That's not what I'm trying to do." Duff raises his hands defensively. "I'm worried about you, female. And if Hermes were awake, he would be too. You're very stressed, and it's not good for the baby."

I pull my hair back and tie it into a messy bun, but random curls drop around my face in protest. "I have plenty of energy. I'm eating, and Bean is kicking up a storm in there. Trust me, I'm fine. Please," I plead again, "can't you do some kind of magic thing to help him? I don't care what it costs."

I don't actually have any gold, but I know that Hermes does, and I'm willing to spend every bit of it if it means he'll wake up and be okay.

HERMES

The fresh and familiar smell of fresh mint and rose breaks into my endless darkness and, keeping my eyes closed, I take in my surroundings.

The angry voice of my female fills my ears, and it takes everything not to smile when I hear it.

Memories of my battle with Leon come back to me, and the moment I knew I was going to die and never hear that beautiful voice again sobers me. *How am I here right now? Am I really alive?*

I wiggle my toes and feel the soft fabric brushing along my skin. I try to swallow, but my tongue is so dry and stuck to the top of my mouth. *How long have I been asleep?*

Picturing Leon's talon ripping me open up the middle of my body, I focus on that area and search for any lingering pain but don't feel anything except skin tightness.

My head hurts a bit though, but nowhere near as bad as it should, because I know I heard my skull crack when I hit the ground. I must have been in some sort of coma or something. My stomach feels empty, and I'm suddenly ravenous.

"What are you even good for?" Havana yells beside me, and I keep very still, not ready to open my eyes just yet because I'm still a little confused.

Matthew's calm but tired voice intervenes, saying, "That's enough. Duff didn't come all this way just for you to get angry with him. I know you're feeling desperate, but it's not his fault."

"I'm sorry, Duff, I'm just worried," Havana says remorsefully, but I'm still surprised about her raising her voice at all.

"Why don't you come and have a coffee with me downstairs, Duff, and after she's finished looking after Hermes and has calmed herself down, you can check out how the baby's doing." Matthew quickly adds, before Havana has a chance to reply, "Not negotiable."

I listen intently as two sets of heavy footsteps leave the room, and my little female sighs sadly beside me.

"Alright, big guy, time for a bath," Havana says to me sweetly, kissing my hand, and my heart melts a little at the contact. "I've gotta take care of my man after all."

The surprise and joy I feel listening to Havana's strong voice has me not wanting to move. I want to lie here and listen to her talking away and relish in it. Havana's voice is so beautiful and sexy; a low, husky kind of voice that always gives me goosebumps.

My body feels relaxed as I hear her walking around, moving things, turning on water in my bathroom and muttering to herself about this or that. For the first time in my life, I feel totally whole in my home. My Kindred is fussing over me in my room, and it feels completely natural.

"Right," Havana says in a firm voice. "Time for a sponge bath. I hope the water's not too warm."

Bath?

The sheet above me gets peeled down to my waist, and I'm shocked when a warm wet cloth starts rubbing circular movements over my warm chest, and it takes every bit of control not to jump at the contact. *Holy shit, she's not only touching me, but washing me.*

Her touch instantly has my body reacting, and not in a way that I can hide.

CHAPTER THIRTY

HAVANA

"Honestly," I mumble, carefully sitting down beside Hermes' bed with the basin of warm water, placing it on the side table. "What good is magic if it doesn't help?"

I slowly lower the sheet covering his impressive chest, folding it at the waist. Hermes has been in the buff since we first cleaned him up because it's a lot easier that way. The first month of sponging him down was definitely different for me. I've never tried to focus on the male body before, but during this task, it's kind of unavoidable. I have been up close and personal with Hermes enough now that I'm no longer shy about what I have to do.

"Right," I tell him. "Time for a sponge bath. I hope the water's not too warm."

Wetting the flannel and squeezing out the extra liquid, I place it on his chest, slowly cleaning him for the day, chatting away at him like I usually do. I wonder if he knows I'm talking to him and can hear my voice. I figure if my baby is able to hear me, then maybe so can Hermes.

Focusing on the job at hand, I tell him all about how frustrated I am that no one has been able to help him and how lonely I am without his company. I clean his chest, face, neck, and arms before moving down to his lower stomach.

Stopping instantly with my hand frozen in the air, I stare down at the tenting sheet below. My eyes go wide at the shocking new development. I've seen him more times than I can count, and I knew he was bigger than anything I've seen before, but right now it looks gigantic.

Wait. *Why the fuck is it doing this now?*

My eyes flick to Hermes' face and see him visually swallow hard, his Adam's apple bobbing with the movement. *Oh, my God. He's awake.* For a second I can't move, the shock rendering me frozen, but then a cheeky smile turns up the corner of my mouth as I realise that he's pretending to be asleep so I don't stop. The thought is surprisingly hot, and I feel my core clench.

Deciding to see how far he'll let me go before he caves, I continue washing him, but more sensually this time, rubbing my fingers more purposefully against his wet skin.

I get up, wet my hands with the soapy water and lean over his body, careful not to let my large baby bump accidentally brush against him. Slowly, I place my hands on the side of his waist, curving them around him. I let them slide down his sides, all the way to his lower hips, the sheet moving down with my movements as I go. Soon, the sheet is only being held up by the large appendage straining beneath it, just like I planned.

I've never felt so brazen before and honestly, don't know what's gotten into me, but the idea that Hermes is enjoying my touch and giving me all the power here does something to me.

Watching his face intently, I wash his hips. One after the

other, slowly and sensually, letting my fingers glide closer and closer to his middle. Hermes' breathing increases and the sheets twitch, but other than that, he shows no sign of giving in, so I up the stakes.

I move the sheet on the left side of his body and put it in between his legs, careful to keep his member covered while I do it, and then I move to his other side, repeating the process. Before long, the only part of his body that's covered is the one part that's struggling to get free.

Unable to help it anymore, I grin and try really hard not to giggle at his amazing restraint. Wetting my hands again, I start from at his feet and rub my way up the inside of his legs, noting his hard swallow as I pass his knees and rise higher and higher up his inner thighs.

As I reach the top of his thighs, I reach over and blow gently on the tender area, at the same time that my thumbs rub right next to his tight balls. His eyes pop open and head tilts down to me, and our eyes meet, his heated gaze scorching me.

I smile up at him cheekily and wink, showing him that I knew he was awake the whole time, and he chokes out a husky laugh. "You wicked minx," he says, shaking his head. "How did you know?"

I look at the distended sheet, twitching with his hard dick, and then back at him, raising an eyebrow. "This," I nod to it, "is new."

Still leaning over, my head way closer to his package than is comfortable for either of us, I blow again, giggling cheekily.

"You better get away from there before he busts free," Hermes chuckles to me, his hands reaching out at the same time for me to go up to him.

Happy to comply, I stand back up and watch with mild fascination as his eyes go saucer wide, taking in my stomach's girth.

"How long was I sleeping?" he asks incredulously, looking utterly confused.

"Three months," I reply with a bit of sass, putting my hands on my hips. "The longest three months of my life. You owe me big time. I was starting to freak out that I was going to have this baby on my own."

I try to make it look like I'm cranky, but in reality, I'm struggling to contain the tears that suddenly threaten to spill over. My relief that Hermes is awake, shaking me to my very core.

"Come here darling," Hermes says softly, his arms even wider. "I'm so sorry. You must have been so scared. I'm here now, and I'll make it up to you every day of my life if you'll let me."

I sniff as a rogue tear strays from me, without permission. Walking over, I fold my body over his, and he pulls me up onto the bed with very little effort, which is astonishing considering he's been in some kind of coma for-freaking-ever.

Positioning my body so that I'm more comfortable with my bump in the way, I snuggle up to him while simultaneously pulling his sheet back up to give him a semblance of privacy. It hasn't missed my notice that he's still as hard as a rock, though.

"Does that hurt?" I ask, looking down at the tented sheet.

Hermes scoffs and replies, "No more than usual."

"Sorry. But honestly, I didn't think that you would go so long without caving," I tell Hermes honestly.

"Me neither," he admits. "I'm sorry for not saying something straight away. At first, I was just trying to get my bearings, and then I didn't want you to stop rambling because I was enjoying the sound of your voice, but when you touched me so tenderly, I was kind of lost, and then it felt so fucking good to be touched after a lifetime without it that I didn't dare to say anything. It was underhanded, and I apologise."

I lean my body up and kiss him softly on the mouth. "You can't be sorry, I'm the one that teased you, and I'm not sorry because it's the first time I've felt in power, and it was kind of hot if I'm going to be honest."

Hermes' body stiffens, and he lets out a big breath. "Trust me, you can do that to me anytime," he chuckles nervously. "The only reason I opened my eyes was because I didn't want to deceive you. My body is yours to do with as you please, little one."

"You're so good to me." I lean into him again, but this time I kiss him deeply, my tongue softly dancing with his. "I missed you."

Hermes groans deeply and grabs the back of my head, bringing my lips back to his, his hunger as deep as mine. Pulling back from me, he pecks me on the nose and smiles sweetly at me, playing with one of my rogue curls. "I missed you every single day, for three hundred and ninety-four years, until my soul found yours, and I'll never let you go again."

"Good, because this is yours now. Take care of it, and I'll take care of yours," I say with a catch in my voice at his beautiful words, placing his hand over my heart and meaning every word.

HERMES

I watch the absolutely perfect vision before me as she walks around my room, picking clothes out of my drawers for me to wear, and my heart soars. If I thought she was stunning before, it's nothing compared to her filled with a babe.

Havana's stomach is round and high in front of her, sitting under a much fuller chest than I remember her having, and her fertile form has my cock twitching and no doubt leaking pre-cum. I've never seen anything sexier in my life.

Her smiling face is radiating beauty, and her skin looks soft and almost like it's glowing. Pregnancy suits her.

"So, how far along are you now?" I ask, sitting up in the bed with my back against the headboard, unsure of the timeline of things.

Havana tilts her head in thought and says, "Mmm, seven months round about. I feel further along, though, my stomach is huge." She rubs it unconsciously and then continues on in her task, humming away at herself.

Exhaustion rides me hard, and I have a splitting headache, but I don't want to close my eyes and miss anything. I've been asleep long enough, and it's time for me to shake it off and get on with things.

A knock sounds at the door, startling her, and she squeaks in surprise. "Oh, my gosh." Havana's eyes go wide, and she walks quickly to the door. "I forgot."

Swinging the door open wide, Havana happily cries out to Duff and Matthew, who are standing there looking confused.

Matthew's appearance takes me aback. His normally pale skin, much paler than usual, and his eyes look lifeless and broken. *What the hell happened while I was asleep?* He looks past Havana and gasps at me sitting up in bed, stepping into the room.

"Brother, you're really awake?" he asks, as if he can't really believe his own eyes, and his heavy tone has worry filling me.

I frown deeply at him as he approaches, stopping at my bedside. I look at Havana and see her looking at Matthew with the same concern as me. "What's going on?" I ask, not wanting small talk, if there's something bigger at play that I need to worry about.

Matthew sits down beside me and smiles weakly. "Nothing that can't wait for now. I swear. How are you feeling?" he asks, redirecting the conversation, but I let him, sensing that whatever it is should be a private talk between just the two of us.

"My head hurts, and I'm fucking starving," I tell him, and my stomach growls on cue.

Duff comes up beside Matthew and slaps my shoulder. "I told your Kindred that she had nothing to worry about, but it never stopped her from calling me up here every week to tell her the same thing over and over again. How about a little pain relief? On the house," he asks, his hands glowing blue.

"Please," I agree, letting him place his hands on the side of my head and close my eyes as the light filters through me, instantly relieving the thumping tension that was drilling in my head. "Thanks."

"How about Havana and I go downstairs and get you something to eat while Matthew here fills you in on what's been going on," Duff suggests and then gives Havana a hard look. "Maybe now she'll let me check her over and see to the health of her and the baby."

I give Havana a questioning look, but she just gazes around the room, purposely not meeting my eyes, and I don't miss the red tinge to her cheeks.

"I think that sounds like a great idea," I say helpfully. "Then afterwards you can tell me all about it, little one. I'd feel a lot better knowing how you were both feeling after being checked out properly." It's a low blow playing on my condition, but I don't feel the slightest bit bad if it means her taking care of herself and not me for a change. I have the distinct feeling that she's been by my side non-stop.

Havana comes over and kisses my bristly cheek. "I'll get you some soup that I made last night," she says before walking to the door.

"And you'll get looked at, right?" I ask, and she pauses mid-stride. "Darling?"

With a huff, she nods, and Duff follows her out with a little chuckle.

I love that female so much it hurts sometimes, and I couldn't be more lucky to have such an incredible Kindred take such good care of me. I don't know what I did to deserve her, but I'll do it again a million times over if it means keeping her.

CHAPTER THIRTY-ONE

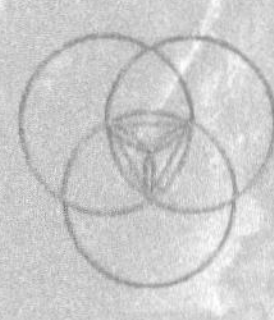

HAVANA

Duff carefully presses on my belly with his hands, a soft blue glow emanating from them as I lay quietly on the large couch. His fingers splay the larger mass, and he tilts his head to the side as if he's listening to something, and I stare at him with fascination.

With a small nod, he lets go and sits back, smiling down at me. "I don't feel any cause for concern. Your baby seems completely healthy, considering everything you've been through. Do any of your scars bother you?"

I self-consciously pull my sleeves further over my wrists. "They don't hurt anymore, if that's what you mean," I answer. Physically, they don't bother me at all anymore because I healed pretty quickly and without issue, but mentally, it still shocks me when I look in the full-length mirror of my bathroom at the remnants of what I've been through. I will forever be reminded of Leon; dead or alive, he lives on in the memories of my skin.

Duff pats my hand gently and says, "You've got this female. Don't let lines on your skin define how you see yourself. You are strong, you are loved, and you're about to be a mother. Scars are nothing but a past that'll never repeat."

I nod and clear my throat, trying to get rid of bubbling emotions that I don't want to deal with right now. "How about some soup?" I ask, needing to be distracted.

"Um, no, thank you," Duff politely declines, looking uncomfortable.

"I cooked the meat properly this time; you won't get sick again," I defend, thinking about the last unfortunate time I fed him. I didn't mean to make him sick.

He gathers his things while saying, "It's not that. I just have a long walk ahead of me, and I have to get home, but tell Hermes I'll be back in three days to give him a more thorough work-over."

Before I can insist, Duff practically runs out of the front door. Jeez, tough crowd. Shrugging my shoulders, I go to the kitchen and fill a big bowl of soup after heating it up. I'm sure Hermes will like it.

With one step in front of the other, I slowly make my way up the stairs, trying not to spill the soup. Things like this are a little harder than they used to be because I can't see my feet anymore. It's crazy how far out my stomach is already.

Luckily, Hermes' bedroom door is open, but as I walk through, the morose atmosphere lets me know that Matthew has told Hermes about what happened to Scooby.

With a low voice, I announce, "I got you some soup. Do you want me to get you some too, Matthew?"

Wiping his eyes, Matthew gets up, offering me the chair he was sitting on. "I'm actually going to rest for a little while. I'm feeling a bit tired, but thank you anyway." Without looking back, he leaves us alone in the room.

Hermes looks at me with dark eyes all over my body, clearly looking for something. His jaw clenches and unclenches with renewed anger. "What did he do to you?" His voice comes out as a low growl.

Not wanting to delay the inevitable, I decide to get to the point. "Leon hurt me a lot, and I have the scars to prove it, but I need you to not linger on it for my mental health." I put the soup on the table beside him and roll the sleeves up on my dress with shaky hands and show him the mangled marks left behind from the shackles I wore.

I don't lift my eyes to look at Hermes, not wanting to see pity or disgust there, as I slowly stand up. Grabbing a hold of my dress, I pull it up high enough to show him the scars on my thighs and cringe at what I know should come next. Dropping the dress back down, I begin to unbutton the top buttons on my high-necked dress until I reach mid-cleavage. For a moment, I just focus on my breathing, giving myself the courage to show the morbid smile forever on my chest.

"Havana?" Hermes questions softly at my pause, but I ignore it and open up my collar, displaying my new marks quietly. My face turned away. "Look at me, little one."

I exhale sharply and look down at him, shocked by what I find in his eyes. Love, acceptance, and understanding glimmers in his gaze, and not an ounce of pity or disgust.

"You are beautiful. Every single inch of you," Hermes tells me honestly. "Sit by me." He scooches over on the bed to make more room for me beside him, and I happily sit with him, leaving my collar open.

Grabbing my hand, Hermes places it on the top of his chest, where his own jagged scar lives. He presses the tip of my fingers on it and slides them all the way down to the bottom of his stomach. "Do you think less of me because of this?" he asks me in a low voice.

I shake my head instantly. "Of course not."

"Then you already know how I feel about yours," he says frankly, and his message hits home. "I will wear this scar proudly for the rest of my existence because it is a story I lived through. This mark represents my strength and love for you, and I would gladly go through it again and again to have you beside me right now."

Leaving my hand on his lower stomach, Hermes raises his hand to my exposed collarbone and traces along my scar with reverence. "Wear it with pride because you're a warrior and this mark represents the love you have for our child and your unending courage to keep going, regardless of what you've been through."

Hermes grabs my chin with tenderness and brings my face to his, looking deeply into my eyes. "I've never been more proud of anyone, and I love you with all that I am. Both of you."

Our kiss is slow and luxurious as we take our time remembering each other and sharing in our memories. I let it wipe away all of my self-doubt and hesitation until I'm drowning in Hermes and everything he means to me.

With one last kiss, I smile up at him and pat his chest lovingly. "It's time for you to eat your kai, before it gets cold."

I reach over and pass Hermes his bowl of soup, feeling very proud of myself for making it without any help. Matthew and I have been taking turns cooking for each other, and it hasn't always been successful on my part, but I've definitely improved.

Hermes takes it from me and swirls the spoon in the bowl, mixing it all together a bit better. His face is unreadable as he sniffs at it, flicking his eyes over to me, and I nod in approval, hoping he'll like it.

He scoops up a big spoonful and brings it to his mouth. The moment his mouth closes around the spoon, he freezes before taking the empty spoon out and returning it to the bowl, his mouth still frozen.

"What's wrong?" I ask, worried that he's in pain.

I watch closely as Hermes' Adam's apple bobs as he swallows the mouthful without chewing, and he starts to cough violently. I quickly pass him the glass of water beside the bed, and he drinks it all down fast.

Clearing his throat, he passes me back the empty glass. "Thank you," he says with an odd tone to his voice.

"You have to chew," I exclaim, slightly concerned. "You can't just swallow a whole mouthful without chewing it first; it's a chunky soup, and you haven't eaten in months. Do you want me to feed you?"

"No," he says quickly, voice slightly higher than usual. "I mean, no, thank you. I'm not as hungry as I thought I was."

Hermes' stomach uses that moment to loudly protest, and I frown at him. "Is something wrong with the soup?" I question with my head tilted to the side.

I watch as the corner of Hermes' lips twitch until he bursts out in sudden hysterics, bending over and trying not to spill the soup. I take it from him and smile at his sudden outburst. I have no idea what's so funny, but he looks so freaking gorgeous when he laughs; his entire face lights up with happiness.

"I'm sorry," he chuckles between bouts of laughter. "I couldn't help it."

"Are you gonna let me in on what's so funny?" I ask, smiling happily.

Hermes pulls at his ear and looks out his large glass balcony doors. "Uh, well," he starts, looking distinctly uncomfortable. "It's just that, I was surprised by the taste of the soup."

"The soup?"

"What was in it?" Hermes asks, looking back at me with a cocked brow. "Did I taste licorice and lamb, and maybe," he smacks his lips together. "Lavender?"

My eyes light up. "Yeah, I remember I once had a lavender ice cream, and it was delicious, so I thought it would be a nice herb to add. Plus, everyone likes licorice," I announce proudly.

"I appreciate how much thought you put into it, my darling, but..." Hermes starts cautiously, clearing his throat again. "Those flavours don't really match each other. But," he adds when my smile drops, "I'd be happy to show you how to use them in other ways. Thank you for being so sweet."

I screw my face up, "Is it that bad?"

Hermes chuckles. "Yes, it really is. I'm sorry. Perhaps leave the cooking to me until you have a better grasp on mixing flavours."

I can't help but smile at him because he's trying so hard not to make me feel bad over something that he clearly thinks is too gross to eat. "You're too good to me, you know that, right?"

Reaching out, he pulls me into his chest with one big arm while placing his other hand on the round of my stomach. "I can't believe how prominent your belly is now." Bean kicks his hand a few times and Hermes' eyes light up, looking down at it. "He's saying hello," Hermes says, elated.

"We've missed you," I say, placing my hand over his, and we lay like that for some time before I accidentally fall asleep wrapped up in his arms, with not a bad dream in sight.

CHAPTER THIRTY-TWO

HAVANA

Soft touches gliding down my back wake me from a deep sleep, and my eyes flutter open to reveal the tattooed face I've grown to love. Hermes' eyes are hooded and soft, taking in all of my features while his hand strokes my back sweetly.

"I didn't mean to wake you," Hermes says, kissing the tip of my nose.

I snuggle my body closer into his side and nuzzle his cheek. "It's okay, I don't mind. Would it be okay if I stay in your room with you now? I don't want to be alone anymore, and it's nice to wake up in your arms."

"It would be my honour, Kindred. If I had my way, we'd never be apart again."

I brush my fingers up and down his chest, drawing invisible lines along his scar and myriad of tattoos, wondering how to brooch the subject I want to talk about.

"What is it, little one?" Hermes asks. "I can hear your brain ticking away."

Kissing the pec' my head's leaning on, I slowly circle his nipple and love the shiver it renders out of him. My eyes look up at him, and I do it again before moving my hand down to where the sheet is folded over and tented again.

Hermes stops my hand before it lowers under the sheet and looks at me questioningly. "Are you sure you want to do that?" he asks me in a husky tone.

I nod and bravely say, "There are a lot of things I'd like to do when you're up for it. I think we've waited long enough, and I want to be claimed by you properly because I'm yours, and I want the whole world to know it."

"You don't need to do that to be mine, Havana," Hermes tells me warmly.

"Maybe not, but I want to. Don't you? I will wait as long as you need to get better again, but I want you to think about it." Nervousness fills me that Hermes might reject my advances. Just because it's something I want, it doesn't mean that he does.

"Trust me, I want to." Hermes adjusts himself. "That's not the issue; I want to make sure that you're ready and want it one hundred percent. It's supposed to be a special thing between Kindreds, and I don't want your past experiences to taint it for us."

"Do you know the weird thing, I don't even think about that stuff when I'm close to you, which is why I know that you will keep me safe and that I don't need to be afraid," I reply, honestly. "Plus, this pregnancy has made me feel a need that I never had before, and I'd very much like you to take the edge off." I smile at him cheekily and rub my thighs together because even the thought of it has me getting wet.

Hermes groans at my admission and sniffs the air. His pupils widen, and his eyelids get heavy. "You smell incredible right now."

His voice rumbles, sending tingles straight between my legs, and I rub my thighs together again. "If you keep doing that, I'll be claiming you sooner rather than later."

I pull my hand out of Hermes' grip and lower it, grasping his thick as fuck dick over the sheet. His hips buck, and he moans deeply, placing his hand on top of mine and moving both of our hands together to rub him up and down. I curl my hands around him tighter, and he moans again.

"Whenever you're well enough," I whisper, leaning up and taking Hermes' lips with mine while still stroking him through the sheet.

"Fuck," he groans on my lips. "I'm already well enough. Can't you tell." He rolls his hips up again.

I blink at him and ask, "Are you sure? You don't want to eat first?"

His lips turn up in a wicked smile. "Oh, I'm gonna eat first. Don't you worry about that."

Hermes sits up and lifts me up like I weigh nothing, sliding me under the sheets with him. With slow, tender movements he undoes the buttons on the front of my dress, all the way down, and before he opens it to view my body in the soft morning light, says to me, "Tell me to stop at any time and I will. You're in charge here. Remember that." I nod, and he opens my dress wide, helping me slip my arms out of the sleeves, and sliding the dress out from under me, throwing it on the ground beside the bed.

"You're so perfect," Hermes says with love, leaning down and kissing my belly. "So beautiful. So sexy."

I lean up and undo my bra clasp behind me, sliding it down my arms and my heavy breasts fall out of the fabric. Hermes looks so hungry when he stares at them that I feel devoured already.

"May I?" he asks, practically drooling.

I lie down on my back with a whole garden of butterflies in my belly and grab Hermes' hand, bringing it down onto my heavy breast, my heart hammering so hard that I'm surprised he can't hear it. I'm not scared, though, just nervous.

Even though Hermes has such huge hands, he handles me with care as he caresses me and learns every curve, as if he's stamping it on his memory. I notice him watching my body's cues to see if I like it or not, and he's encouraged with every arch and moan I make. The feel of him stroking my nipples a certain way feels so good that my core floods more every time, wanting him to touch me there.

Hermes' eyes meet mine as he lowers his head slowly, licking his lips seductively before taking my pebbled nipple into his mouth. He nips at it and tongues it in a way that pulses my pussy, the ache there growing almost painfully.

"Oh, God," I cry out, grabbing his braids and holding him close, not wanting him to stop what he's doing. "That feels so good."

Hermes' beard brushes the underside of my sensitive breast, increasing the torturous assault to my senses. "I've only just started, my love," he says over my wet nipple. The warm air of his breath blows over the sensitive nub, and I shiver.

The hand currently on my other breast lowers, trailing a soft touch over my round belly and down to my underwear. Instead of dipping inside them, his fingertips slowly slide over the top, down to my slit, and I open my legs wide, enjoying the way they trail over my most sensitive place.

"Fuck, you're so wet that you've soaked your panties," Hermes growls out, nipping at my nipple harder, making me squirm.

He rubs his fingers up and down and the friction is so freaking good, and I moan out loud, my head pushing back into the pillow. "More," I plead, "Please."

With a pop, Hermes lets go of my nipple and raises his body

next to mine, positioning himself on his knees and grabs both sides of my underwear, looking at me for permission. I nod and lift my hips up as he slides them down my body; the sheet falling away from both of us at the movement.

I look down at his cock and wonder how the heck *that's* supposed to fit inside me without hurting. Noticing my worried glance, Hermes leans down and kisses me softly.

"I promise that I won't hurt you. There are ways to make this feel amazing. Do you trust me?" he asks.

Reaching down bravely, I wrap my small hand around his girth, the best that I can, in response. "I trust you."

"You know, I'm getting kind of hungry now," he says, surprising me, and I quirk an irritated brow at him. "I might have my breakfast now." He chuckles at my annoyed face but situates himself between my thighs and looks me over like I'm a buffet of everything he loves most.

Hermes lowers himself between my legs so that I can't see him properly over my belly, and I blush furiously at the intimacy of the move, feeling really exposed.

Before I get a chance to ask what he's doing, I feel him kiss the crease of my leg, extremely close to the ache driving me mad, and I clench my pussy tight at the contact. Another kiss lands on the outside, and all I think of is that I want it closer. He's so close, but so far.

I feel his fingers brush along my outer lips, pulling them open, and his warm breath on my core makes me plead, "Please."

Without making me wait even a second, his lips find my pulsing nub and suck it in, making me cry out at the intense feeling. He sucks on it like candy and then moves his mouth further down, his tongue exploring my wet slit, licking every inch of me, while his thumb lazily strums my clit.

"Oh, my God," I cry out as a fantastic sensation builds tighter and tighter, making me pant wildly and needing more.

Taking my cries as some kind of cue, Hermes brings his tongue back up to my clit and starts swirling it in a way that has my eyes rolling into the back of my head, and my fingers reach down for his hair, grasping desperately at the braids I can reach.

Suddenly, my pussy fills with a large digit, and he works it in and out; the wet sounds it makes should embarrass me, but I'm so caught up in how fucking good it feels that I couldn't care less. He adds another one and then another, his attack on my clit never ceasing.

The mixture of his mouth devouring me and his large fingers stretching and pumping in me mercilessly become too much, and I scream loud as something inside me snaps. The ecstasy drowns me as my eyes squeeze tight, my back arched and toes curling.

I've never felt anything like it, and my body shudders and shakes while Hermes licks me softly a few more times until I can see properly again. His fingers slowly keep pumping, and he raises himself back up, taking my nipple back into his mouth and then grinning up at me like a Cheshire cat.

"Now, that's what I call the most important meal of the day," Hermes jokes, sliding beside me so that he doesn't put any weight on my tummy. "Do you want more, darling, or would you like to stop here?" he asks me thoughtfully.

"I want all of you, right now," I demand, nowhere near done.

Chuckling, Hermes turns my body so that I'm on my side. "I think it will be best to do it this way because of this little fella," he explains, scooching his body behind mine so that he's the big spoon, and he rubs my belly lovingly.

I let him manoeuvre my body so that my top leg is open and above his, and I feel his impressive length pressing against my opening. The thrill that I'm finally going to be his in every way overshadows any doubts that might want to pop up. I'm so ready for this.

Hermes kisses my neck as he uses his hand to push himself inside; the large head of his cock breaches my entrance, and I'm pleasantly surprised that it doesn't hurt at all, it only feels tight. He starts to push in a little more and a slight burn begins to build at the pressure, but before I can worry about it, his magical fingers start rubbing against my clit in soft circular motions, distracting me from any pain with extreme pleasure.

"Yeah, like that," I tell him between pants, and before I know it, he's fully seated inside me.

"You okay, darling?" Hermes asks me, his voice sounding needy and hot as hell.

I roll my hips back and forth, enjoying the growls he makes at the movement. "I want you to claim me. Make me yours and fill me up." I have no idea where this temptress came from, but my inner Goddess just showed up, and she's hungry for more.

With one hand tightly clasping my hip and the other one curled under my neck and grasping my breast gently, his own hips begin to move, filling me over and over again. The feeling is so intense that my leg shakes, and my ass grinds further back to get him even deeper.

Hermes nips at my ear and moves his hand back to my pussy, rubbing against me in perfect rhythm with his hips. He starts pistoning into me harder and harder and the ecstasy builds higher again, and I cry out, needing more.

My hips meet his with a fury neither of us were expecting, the pleasure so unbelievable that I can't keep in my moans, completely uncaring if anybody can hear me.

"Cum for me again," Hermes growls sexily in my ear and pinches my clit hard.

Unexpectedly, I scream out, my pussy pulsing as he drives me over the edge. Hermes fucks me even harder as I do, and in seconds cries out his own release, filling me up in every way.

We lay there panting and my leg drops as I try to catch my breath, his cock still deep inside me; and I've never been more content than I am right now.

"Holy shit," Hermes murmurs sleepily. "That was even better than I thought it would be."

I giggle. "That was kind of amazing," I say, blushing.

"Kind of?" he asks. "Obviously, I wasn't doing it right then. I'd better try again, just to be sure."

With his big dick twitching inside me, he rolls his hips, and I turn to him with a look of amazement. "Can you do that again so soon?" I ask.

"I'm a Drake, little one. You'd be surprised what I can do," Hermes tells me huskily, beginning to fuck me again, and I couldn't be happier.

CHAPTER THIRTY-THREE

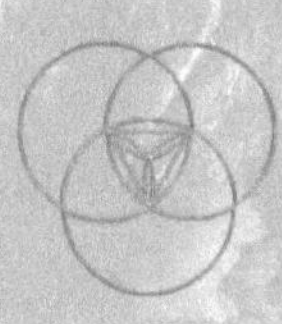

HERMES

After the best day of my freaking life, Havana and I finally make it downstairs because I really am starving now.

I surprisingly haven't had any issues since waking up from my three-month sleep, if you can call it that. My energy went up naturally, and my head hasn't bothered me since Duff sorted it out. After the last twenty-four hours I've had, I would've expected to be more exhausted, but instead I'm motivated and ready to take on the world.

Holding Havana's hand, we head into the lounge to find Matthew sitting there, reading a book. When we walk through the threshold, his head pops up and a knowing smirk lines his face. With all the noises of ecstasy my Kindred made, there's no way he didn't hear what was going on, but even if he hadn't, he'd smell the evidence as soon as we walked into the room. We may have showered, but that won't take away the scent of me finally claiming her.

"Hello there, lovebirds," Matthew greets us, instantly painting Havana's cheeks the pink that I adore. "I take it her soup didn't kill you?"

Unable to help myself, I laugh out loud at that, earning myself a fake scowl from my love. "I didn't eat it."

"Smart male," Matthew retorts, and Havana lets go of my hand, putting her fists on her hips.

"It's not *that* bad," she disagrees, but Matthew and I just laugh harder. "You guys suck."

Matthew points to the kitchen. "I made a bunch of sandwiches when I heard you two moving around upstairs. I figured you'd be hungry after your workout." He winks at us, and Havana goes even brighter.

"You're adorable," I say to her, kissing her cheek softly. "Sit down, and I'll get us some of those sandwiches. Thanks, brother." He wasn't wrong. I was hungry beforehand, but I'm famished now.

Before eating, Matthew takes me aside quickly to give me something that he was holding onto for me, and I'm forever grateful because I thought I'd lost it; Havana's ring.

We enjoy our lunch together, and they catch me up on all the things I missed while I slept. I enjoyed watching the two of them laughing about this or that because I get the distinct feeling that not a lot of laughter was to be had until now.

"Come for a walk with me?" Havana asks, standing up and offering me her hand. "There's something I want to show you."

Curious, I happily accept her hand, and we take a stroll together out the front. Her small hand feels so delicate in mine, and I can't help but to think about how lucky I am that she's chosen to trust me and accept me as her Kindred.

We walk into the garden that we both love and Havana happily drags me along to her favourite spot where a cute, fluffy audience waits for her. She sits down in front of them, and I follow suit, happy to see my little friends are safe and well. However, they all seem to have tiny little versions of themselves huddling around them.

"Look, they all have babies too," Havana announces proudly, patting the cute baby bunnies by her feet. "I love all the floofs," she all but squeals.

Reaching over, I rub her belly again, unable to go very long without my hands on it. "I wonder what they're gonna think when we bring our little floof?" I ask, looking forward to the day when I get to meet our son.

With my other hand, I reach into my pocket and pull out the ring that I had carefully crafted for Havana before everything went wrong, and turn to face her on my knees.

"While this isn't something we normally do in Rathe, I wanted to make an effort to show you how much you mean to me, little one." I grab her tiny hand and slip on the diamond band as she sucks in a shocked breath. "Be my Kindred. Be my wife. Be my life. I will love you and protect you for as long as the world's turn."

Havana's other hand covers her mouth and tears spring to her eyes as she whispers, "Yes. Forever, yes."

LIFE IS BUT A DREAM. A perfect dream, it would seem.

Every week that passes by with Havana by my side is better than the last, whether it's in the garden, sharing in a laugh, or snuggled up in our bed. I've always thought of myself as a happy male, but I never truly knew what happiness was until now.

My hand glides over the bulging globe that holds my baby

safe inside and I watch as it morphs before my eyes. Our son is usually active, but these days there's not enough space left for him to move around, so with each movement now, her entire stomach shifts. It looks painful sometimes, but she promises me that it isn't.

"Oh," Havana humphs, shifting her body slightly. "I'm ready for him to evacuate now. Your lease is up, buddy, time to leave," she groans, clearly uncomfortable.

She had the worst sleep ever last night and has been uncomfortable all day, more than normal anyway. Now that it's time to sleep again, she looks exhausted, but also like she's still too uncomfortable to sleep.

"You need to rest, darling," I tell her, worried. "Just close your eyes and get as much sleep as you can."

"Easy for you to say," Havana grumbles at me, not appreciating my input. "I've had the worst freaking day. My Braxton Hicks pain has been non-stop, and I'm over it."

She chews on her lip as it starts to tremble, her eyes filling with moisture.

"What's wrong?" I ask her, taking her hand into mine. "Are you in pain? Do you want me to tell Matthew to get Duff?"

"It's just," she says sniffing, "What if I'm a bad Mum? What if I screw it up, or he hates me? What if I can't keep him safe?"

I pull her into my arms and cradle her close. "My darling, you're gonna be a great mother and between the two of us, he'll be the safest person in Rathe. You're not worried about me being a dad, are you? Because I swear that, I'll do everything I can to keep you both safe and happy."

"No," Havana tells me, wiping away a rogue tear. "I know you'll be a great dad. I'm just scared and don't want to mess this up."

"We've got this," I tell her confidently, because there's no way

I'm gonna fuck this up, and I have zero doubt that Havana will be the best kind of mum.

Havana groans again, shifting out of my embrace. "Argh, I have to go to the toilet again." She wiggles her butt to the end of the bed, and I give her ass a push to help her up. "Thanks. I'll be glad when I can get out of bed without needing help again."

I watch with a smile as she waddles over to the bathroom. I never want to forget this sight because it's just too damn adorable. She disappears behind the door, and I lean back on the bed, closing my eyes, completely content with the world.

"Fuck," Havana cries out, and my eyes snap open.

"What?" I race from the bed and knock on the bathroom door. "Are you okay? Do you need help?" The door swings open to a wide-eyed Havana, and she looks down at her soaking wet nighty and feet. "Fuck," I parrot. *It's time.*

Oh, my Gods. Oh, my Gods. Oh, my Gods.

My mind goes into meltdown mode, and I start racing for the bedroom door, throwing it open and hollering as loud as I can, "Matthew!" I run down the hall and bang on his bedroom door. "Matthew!"

He opens it with sleepy eyes and takes in my probably disheveled appearance. "What's wrong?"

"You have to go," I state. "Now! Right now! Havana's water broke. We need Duff."

"Breathe, dude, you're hyperventilating," Matthew tells me, grabbing my shoulder. "Where's Havana?"

Holy shit. I left Havana in the bathroom.

Turning around, I run back to the bedroom and find Havana stripping off her soiled nighty and throwing it on the floor of the bathroom. "I'm so sorry. What do you need?" I ask wildly, panic filling me.

Havana looks at me and starts laughing. "It's okay, baby. I'm going to be fine. I just have to get in the bath and wait for Duff. He said he'll portal here when we're ready, so I'm sure it won't take too long if Matthew flies straight there."

I know she's right, but all of a sudden I feel less than ready. Catching my breath, I start filling the bathtub with warm water, reminding myself mentally that everything's alright.

* * *

HAVANA

Getting into the bath isn't as easy as it normally is. The pain and tightening of my stomach has become really frequent and almost unbearable.

I started getting pain early last night, but I thought it was just Braxton Hicks. Apparently, I was wrong because now the pain is no doubt full-blown labour. *I should have called for Duff this morning.*

Not wanting to panic Hermes any more than he already is, I don't tell him how bad it really is because I think I may be closer to giving birth to this baby than I originally thought. As soon as my water broke, I noticed a steady increase of contractions, and they're getting really close together.

I lay my head back on the bath edge, and my stomach begins to tighten again already; I brace myself for the incoming pain, my fingers gripping the edge of the bath tight. I groan and breathe through it, and the bloody thing seems to go on forever.

Opening my eyes, the first thing I see is a pale Hermes leaning over the bath, with his gaze boring into my unclenching belly. "Holy hell, Havana, I can see your contractions." He pales even more at his own words and then looks into my eyes. "Don't lie to me. How bad is it?"

"You need to get a towel, some kind of clamp and scissors in case he comes before Duff gets here," I tell him honestly, needing him to be prepared. "I don't want to worry you, I just want to know that you're ready so that I can relax."

Hermes gets up and practically runs from the bathroom, and I chuckle at how seriously he's taking this. I'm so grateful that he's reliable because I know that even if the party starts a little early, he'll make sure everything's alright.

Another contraction starts up, and I try not to tense up, focusing on keeping my breathing as even as I can. *I can do this.* I look at the marks on my wrist and remind myself that I can get through anything.

By the time it wears off, Hermes is back in the bathroom and turning the large bench into a post-natal station. There's even his little portable bed laid out, ready to go.

"I love you," I tell him as he straightens everything out.

Hermes turns to me and then sits beside me next to the bath, taking my hand into his. "I love you too. So much," he tells me, kissing my temple. "I've got you, darling, and I'm not going anywhere."

With that, my stomach tightens again, and the pain is so intense that I practically growl through it, unable to hide my pain anymore.

Again and again the pain wracks me, tightening my stomach so much that I scream, and Hermes never leaves my side. He massages my lower back when I turn onto my hands and knees and helps me in any way that I demand because I am definitely demanding things now, no longer giving a shit about my manners.

"Aagh." A guttural cry rips from me while I'm leaning on Hermes, my arms wrapped around his neck tightly. "I can't do this," I state, starting to cry, the pain excruciating.

"Yes, you can. You are strong and brave, and you can do this," Hermes tells me, rubbing my lower back the way I showed him.

Pressure pushes down inside me, and I feel like I need to poo, but it hurts. I push, grunting with almost animal noises.

"Are you pushing?" Hermes asks me, his voice serious.

I moan loud, ignoring him because I can't fucking talk right now. After the need passes, I turn my body off Hermes, bending over and leaning against the side of the bath. "I have to," I moan, and start crying again. "Oh, God, it's coming back." I groan deeply and push down, my chin meeting my chest.

"I'm going to put my hand down and feel what's happening," Hermes tells me, but I don't care. All I can feel is pain and pressure and scream.

I feel his large hand down there, and he curses before telling me, "Keep pushing, darling, his head is almost out. I'll catch him. I promise. Everything's okay. You're doing a great job. Push, honey."

And I do. I push so hard that I can't breathe. I remember what I've seen on TV and count to ten slowly before letting it go, and my contraction stops, but the burning pain continues.

"His head's out," Hermes says, his voice breaking with emotion. "I can see his thick black hair through the water."

"Is there anything around his neck?" I ask.

"No, it's all clear," Hermes croaks. "Can you feel him?"

I look down but just see murky water, and I reach my hand between my legs, shocked when I feel a tiny little head sticking out of me, and I suck in a sob. *This is really happening. I'm having a baby.*

The tightening starts again, and I tell Hermes. "Push baby. I've got you," he tells me, and I do.

Holding my breath, I curve my body and count to ten in my head, pushing as hard as I can. I feel a terrible burning pain and then nothing but relief.

"Havana. Holy shit, you did it," Hermes cries out, and I awkwardly turn around, looking in between my legs and finding our baby in his giant hands, floating under the water in total peace.

I reach down and cradle him with my hands too, and we both bring him to the surface, the umbilical cord still inside me.

His perfect little face puckers, and he opens his mouth, taking in his first breath, and I'm blown away that this perfect, tiny person with thick curly black hair just like me came out of me. I'm a mum, and he's a... *she*.

"I hope she likes blue," I chuckle with tears streaming down my cheeks, the pure love for my little angel making my heart grow inside my chest. I sob with happiness.

"She?" Hermes says in shock, getting a better look. "A female? We have a daughter. Shit on a stick, we have a daughter."

Laughter breaks through my tears, and I rest our little princess on my chest, just as her sweet little cries fill the room. Her echo of life brings fresh tears pouring down Hermes' cheeks as he smiles from ear to ear; his hand gently rubbing our daughter's back.

"Can I name her after my mother?" I ask him softly, looking down at our perfect cherub.

Hermes chuckles. "You can call her whatever you like, my queen. I will love her until my dying breath, no matter what her name is." He leans over and kisses us both on the head. His tears joining my own.

"Welcome to the world, Brenda. I will love you in a way my mother never got the chance to, and your daddy will protect you in a way that mine never did." My thumb strokes Brenda's cheek softly. "One day I'll tell you all about your grandma Verna and how you're safe because she was so brave."

"Looks like we missed one hell of a party," Duff says at the bathroom door, with a shocked-looking Matthew beside him. "Congratulations guys."

CHAPTER THIRTY-FOUR

HAVANA

"I can't get over how freaking adorable Brenda is," Summer says before making cooing noises at her as she cradles her close. "How old is she again?"

Hermes smiles wide and pronounces proudly, "Two months today." He wraps his arms around me, sitting on his lap. "Brenda barely even cries, it's amazing."

"Enjoy her sitting still," Reid states, looking down at his eleven-month-old twins waddling around the room. "Once she finds her feet, she'll be into all sorts of trouble. Trust me."

Cheyenne sits on the armchair of her mum's seat, playing with Brenda's little hands. "She's so cute," she says, with her sweet little dimples popping out.

I try to imagine what Brenda will look like at that age and can see her curly black locks tied up in two piggy tails with little ribbons, smiling and playing with Hermes in the garden. It makes me smile, and I can't wait for what the future will bring, but I also don't want her to grow too fast. I absolutely love having a baby in the house, and Hermes is the perfect dad, up all night with her if she's restless and spoiling her rotten with kisses and cuddles during the day.

"Janice and her teddy bears should be here soon," Bell says, laughing at her own joke. "You wait till you see her. She's as big as a house."

"Excuse you." I hear Janice say in her high-pitched voice. "I *am* a house, thank you very much."

I take in my heavily pregnant friend, feeling sorry for her because I can still remember clear as day how uncomfortable you are in your last few weeks, and I know that she's due any day now.

Her eyes light up when she sees Brenda in Summer's arms, and she smiles over at me as she glides into the room. While Janice is nine months pregnant, she's also apparently a pregnancy unicorn. Her long lithe body looks generally untouched by it, except for her stomach; even her ankles still look small.

"Hey, Havana. Congratulations," Janice greets me as kindly as ever, coming over for a hug. I stand so she doesn't have to bend down, and let her hug me as big as she can with the space that she's got. "I've missed you so much. I'm so glad you came for a visit, and how cute is this little pumpernickel," she says, moving over to kiss Brenda on the head. "Oh, she's so freaking precious. Don't you worry now, I'm working on getting her future Kindred out. You'll see, they'll be sweet as pie on each other."

Hermes grumbles. "Hey now, no more talk of my little girl moving on like that. She needs to wait at least a hundred years before she starts talking about Kindreds and things."

"Hear, hear," Blayze adds with a nod, looking down at his own daughter, Mina.

Mina has her daddy's warm skin tone and mummy's thick lips

and warm smile; her happy little face shows an easy-going, carefree personality. Her twin, Demetrius, is completely different with his serious little frown and blond hair. He follows his sister around everywhere, watching everything she does, as Mina runs around without a care in the world. The only thing they have in common is their mama's onyx eyes.

"Would you like a drink, my darling?" Hermes asks me quietly, and I lean back into him.

Kissing him on the cheek, I smile at him. "I'm fine. Thank you," I tell him, and it's not a word of a lie. My life couldn't get any better if I tried.

Brenda starts to fuss, and I feel the milk drop in my breasts. "Time for a feed, baby," I say, getting up and taking Brenda off Summer. "You can have her back when I'm done."

Summer, knowing me well, gets up with me and tells me to follow her. She takes me to their spare room so I can breastfeed in private. I've come a long way, but I'll always be a private person, and I'm very grateful to her for not waiting for me to ask.

"Derryn will be here shortly; he was going in this direction on his way to drop a few girls off to their new locations, and when he heard you two were here with Brenda, he immediately organized a short detour, so he didn't miss out," Summer tells me before she leaves.

Sitting down on the bed, I change her nappy and get Brenda into a better position to feed her and help her latch on. I love this time together. It's a special bonding time that I don't have to share with anyone. Not that I mind sharing her with others, but it's nice to have this.

As I'm finishing up with Brenda, Hermes slips into the room and happily takes her off me while I fix my shirt back into place.

"Hey baby girl, daddy missed you," he says to her in a sweet voice, giving her soft little kisses all over her face. "You're the sweetest little thing. Yes, you are."

I laugh at him. "For a terrifying guy, you're a real softy, you know that?"

We walk out of the room together, with Brenda wrapped up and snuggled in Hermes' giant arms. When we join the others, I'm taken aback by how many people are now in the space. Derryn is talking to his brother, while Nateesha and Alice, along with two other girls I don't recognise, are sitting at various places around the room.

I notice one of the girls I've never seen before is trying to flirt with Blayze, touching his arm and laughing at some random thing. I scowl at the sight and look over to see Summer giving the back of her head daggers. If looks could kill.

Poor Blayze shuffles on the spot uncomfortably, clearly looking for a way out of the conversation, while his Kindred brothers look on, obviously amused at his predicament.

Summer, having had enough of the public display of disrespect, goes to walk over there, but Bell grabs her arm and shakes her head. "I've got this." I see her mouth to Summer with a smile.

Bell walks over and squeezes herself in between them, shocking Blayze, but his eyes light up in understanding almost instantly.

"You can fuck all the way off if you're gonna act like a slut in Summer's house, Mischa," Bell states bluntly. "Keep your fucking hands to yourself, or I'm gonna throw you out on your ass, since Blayze is clearly too polite to."

My mouth drops open at Bell's threat, and I hear Summer and Salvatore both openly chuckling. I almost feel bad for this Mischa girl until she opens her mouth.

"Please," she drawls, heavily accented. "I wouldn't want her sloppy seconds, anyway. I want a man with taste, not one willing to lower himself to the likes of Summer," Mischa scoffs, stepping back out of Bell's space.

Bell's face goes red with anger, and she narrows her eyes, but before she gets a chance to lunge at the woman, Blayze grabs her arm and moves her aside.

"Out!" he demands in a powerful boom, his finger pointed to the front door. "Now!"

Derryn sighs and walks over to them, taking the visibly shaken Mischa by the sleeve, all but dragging her outside. "What did I tell ya? Dinnae open your mouth. For feck's sake." He opens the front door and lightly shoves her out. "You can wait out here now until we're done. Enjoy the cold breeze."

Derryn slams the door in her stunned face and turns to the room, "Sorry bout that. She's been a right pain in my arse."

We have an awesome day, catching up with our old friends. Janice and Summer spend an uncomfortable amount of time swooning over my ring and verbally stating how lucky *I* am. I get the feeling that Janice is dead serious and trying to get the hint into her Bear-men, but Summer just looks like she's messing with hers. The smirk when they're not looking is a dead giveaway. Either way, there's a room full of nervous guys.

Matthew stayed behind at the house, deciding not to come with us. I think he wanted some time on his own, and I can't help but wonder if Scooby was more to him than we initially realised. His grief has been a heavy shadow on our otherwise happy home, not that we'd ever want him to leave. Matthew is family to me now and Godfather to Brenda. If he's going to grieve anywhere, then it should be with us.

Hopping into bed in Summer's spare room, I turn to Hermes and ask in a soft voice, so we don't wake Brenda, "Do you think Matthew's alright?"

"He'll be okay, darling. It'll just take a bit of time. What happened to Scooby hit him really hard, and it's not for us to decide how he needs to grieve," Hermes tells me quietly, curling my hair in his finger.

"Do you think they were in a relationship?" I ask him out loud for the first time.

Hermes sighs deeply. "It wouldn't surprise me. They've been close for a very long time, and it's not uncommon for most males to be in serious relationships here at one time or another. There are hardly any females, remember?"

"I hate that he's in so much pain, but I understand it. I'm glad that he never saw Scooby at the end. It would've killed him," I tell Hermes honestly. We sit quietly for a minute, lost in our own memories, and then I decide to change the subject, not wanting that image in my head for a second longer. "What was with that Mischa chick?"

Hermes laughs. "Ah, yes. Mischa ruffled a few feathers back in Threshold too, if I remember correctly; but I get the distinct feeling that she and Summer specifically don't like each other. I feel bad for Alice. She's gonna be living with her for a while, by the looks of it."

"Maybe she's just lonely and wants to be loved," I say, thinking about it. "It's not easy to feel alone in a big new world."

I turn around and back into Hermes, wanting his arms to enfold me, and he whispers in my ear, "You're very kind, my Kindred, and I'm so proud that you're mine."

"Arianna seemed nice. I've always loved the Spanish accent. It's so pretty," I say, closing my eyes as he pulls me in closer, his hard dick digging in my ass.

I give a little wiggle and laugh quietly as he groans into my neck. "If you keep doing that, I'm not going to let you sleep."

* * *

HERMES

"Maybe I'm not tired yet," my cheeky female says to me in the husky voice that drives me crazy.

Grinding into her more, I revel in her small curves, as my hands trace along her body. This perfect tiny creature is the sexiest fucking thing in all of Rathe, and she's all mine.

"You know," I start with a growl, taking her earlobe between my teeth and lowering my hand to her already flat stomach, the Kindred claim keeping her body in the condition she will stay in for hundreds of years. "I think it's not a terrible idea to practice for a sibling for Brenda," I say, half as a joke and half because I want to have as many little Brenda's with her as she'll give me.

Havana chuckles low. "I bet you would. You just like my body rounded with child, don't you?" she asks, hitting the nail on the head.

"Maybe."

Havana turns around and pushes me onto my back, and I happily comply. "Well, in that case," she says, stripping off her large nightshirt and leaving her bare for me. "We'd better get to work."

She straddles me and rubs her already moist pussy up and down my length, and I'm happy as fuck that I sleep in the nude. I grab her hips and grind her along me.

"Fuck, you feel good," I moan, and she takes my cock in her hand, lifting herself higher while sliding it along her soaking slit.

With little movements, she begins to slide down my dick, the little minx a pro at working my length inside her tight cunt now. I growl, with my fingers tightening on her hips. The visual of her gliding down me from above is so fucking hot I want to cum now, and I'm not even all the way inside her yet.

"It's gonna feel even better in a minute," she groans, pushing me all the way home. Her head falls back in pleasure, and I stroke her little nub the way she likes it till she mewls and starts to ride me slowly; her juices practically dripping down my length every time she lifts herself up.

"That's it darling. Take it all," I tell her, letting her be in full control while she rides me, knowing she loves it that way.

Leaning over, she nips hard at my bottom lip, then kisses me hard, her tongue delving into my mouth and her hips speed up. Slamming up and down, our combined moans quiet because of Brenda.

"Fill me up baby, I want every drop if we're going for number two," Havana whispers to me, panting in a way that tells me she's close to her release, and I increase the pressure of my finger on her clit. I'm so fucking turned on that she wants my baby inside her that my balls tighten painfully.

Pinching her nub when I know she's ready. She muffles her scream with my mouth, and it sends me straight into my own orgasm as her pussy strangles my dick, milking it for all it's got.

Havana collapses on top of me with heavy breaths, and I wrap my arms around her, kissing the top of her wild hair. "That should do it," I joke, and we hold each other like that until she falls asleep atop me, with me still nestled deep inside.

EPILOGUE

ALICE

We finally get to our destination, and I'm so done with walking. I didn't get this amazing plus-sized physique by working out; I tell myself bitterly.

My weight has always been my biggest flaw, but I don't seem to be able to stop eating. I love food, and I hate exercise; it's just the way it is. I want to be better, but I also don't want to have to change who I am and what I love, food.

It certainly doesn't help my self-love when I'm surrounded by a world filled with supermodels and bodybuilders. What a way to fuck with me.

I turn and look at my travelling companion, Mischa; she's a real piece of work. She has nothing to say to me other than how fat I am and how I should be disgusted with myself. To make matters worse, she's probably the hottest chick I've ever seen, and she's human.

"You're gonna love it here," Derryn tells us as we approach the gorgeous, wooden village in the middle of a wide, grass plain. Wild flowers grow all around and the whole place looks like a cute old western. "The Cheetahs are proud males, and they take good care of their own, and while you're here, you'll be treated like family."

He looks darkly at Mischa. "Dinnae be a cock up while you're here. They dinnae deserve your special brand of sass."

She gives him a fake smile that instantly turns into a real one when a blond, Henry Cavill look-alike, and Salem, the receptionist from the doctor's office in Threshold, stride over to us. The two of them take my breath away; they're so fucking pretty.

Great. More pretty people.

Mischa slows down and drops back to where I'm walking and smirks at me cruelly, "Well, well, well. Look at the men here, aren't they something? I think I'm going to like it here. I bet I'll find my Kindred with a sexy Cheetah." She looks me up and down in the way she does, that tells me how ugly she thinks I am. "Sucks to be you. It's a shame there's no one in Rathe suitable for someone like you. You never know, maybe there are mole shifters. Then you don't have to worry about them seeing you."

With a boisterous laugh at my expense, she speeds up her steps, putting an exaggerated sway in her small hips, and says in a loud, saucy voice to the approaching men, "Hello boys, I'm Mischa, and it's a *pleasure* to make your acquaintance." She pronounces pleasure in her sexy Russian accent, extra thick, and I want to gag.

Unfortunately, I also want to hide because both sets of the Cheetah's eyes ignore her and fall solely on me. Their focused gazes trailing my body from top to bottom, and my stomach drops at their attention.

Please don't notice how fat I am.

"Alice?" Salem asks, recognising me. "I thought that was you. This is Baxter. Welcome to your new home."

Home? Yeah right, with the dirty look that Mischa just gave me for stealing her limelight, I doubt very much that this is going to be as simple as that.

ACKNOWLEDGMENTS

Husband, your constant support gets me through my biggest hurdles and I love you endlessly for it. Thank you for always being you.

Wifey of my lifey, this book is for you babe. I know how much you love a big serving of Hermes. Enjoy.

I want to say thanks to two groups of people that have made my journey as an author amazing. The people who support me and help me to become a better writer every time. My writing team and my readers.

To my fan-fucking-tastic Alpha/Beta team, you are a bunch of irreplaceable queens and I am infinitely grateful to have you on my team. Sandy, Tash, Laura, Marissa, Ever, Ashley, Amanda and Taneisha. Talk about a dream team. Thank you for all your time, energy and encouragement.

My readers, without you I am just a crazy person with notes of notes and voices in my head. Haha. I literally can not do this without you and I appreciate every single one of you. It brings me so much joy to hear from you and how much you have enjoyed my stories because I do this for you. I put my blood, sweat and many tears into making these books the best I can to bring you a piece of my soul and make you happy. You are loved. You are important. You are everything. Thank you for your ongoing love and support.

A big shout out as well to my PA, my editor, and my cover

designer. I worship at your feet, you wonderful humans. Thanks for helping me bring magic to the masses.

ABOUT THE AUTHOR

Hi, I'm Alexandra, an Aussie/Kiwi mother of three, married to the best husband around.

My life is surrounded by lots of animals because I just can't say no to all their cuteness. I have a rare chronic illness that keeps me grateful for the beauty that life brings and my pen name is in honour of my amazing Grandparents who are everything to me.

My soul lives off coffee, family, reading, storms, good scotch and great wine, mountains, and is a real knowledge whore.

I'm a firm believer in being kind to others because it *does* matter, and it *does* make a difference. If I can make just one person happy with my stories or even give them a reprieve they may desperately need to escape their harder reality, then I've done my job right.

My imagination is a constantly growing paradise for me and I feel blessed that I get to share a little of it with you.

Thank you for coming on my journey with me; You *are* appreciated.

If you have enjoyed my story, please take the time to leave me a review on amazon. Reviews are the bread and butter of indy authors and everyone counts.

Here are some links to my social media accounts:

Facebook Group:

https://www.facebook.com/groups/alexandrasguardians

Facebook Page:

https://www.facebook.com/Alexandra.K.Martin.Books

Amazon:

https://www.amazon.com/Alexandra-K-Martin/e/B08NHK4JC4/

Instagram:

https://instagram.com/alexandra.k.martin.books?igshid=1m508hfimy8zz

Goodreads:

https://www.goodreads.com/author/show/20962962.Alexandra_K_Martin

Newsletter

https://mailchi.mp/27cd881447ed/alexandrakm-nl

Tiktok:

https://vm.tiktok.com/ZSeM3U4HQ/

Website to come...

OTHER BOOKS BY ALEXANDRA K. MARTIN

Series

Rathe Chronicles (Epic Fantasy Romance)

-Summer's Confine, Book One (RH)

-Janice's Entanglement, Book Two (Menage)

-Havana's Hell, Book Three (MF)

-Alice's Coalition, Book Four (RH)(Coming 2022)

Standalones

-Broken Faun (Paranormal RH/ Coming Mar 2022)

Collaboration/Standalone

-Lust: A Golden Bird Retelling. Sinners Fairytales Collaboration, Book Six (Dark Contemporary RH)

Anthologies

-Hidden Fate (RH), featured in 'Rebirth of the Dark Hunter' (Urban Fantasy/ Coming Feb 2022)

-Dom X (MF), featured in 'My Perfect Pleasure' (Erotic/ Coming May 2022) CO-WRITE as SOULSISTERS

Coming on the 12th of March, 2022. Broken Faun.

Pre-order link: https://books2read.com/brokenfaun

Looking for new books to read? Try 'Gluttony' by Kira Roman

Pre-order link: https://books2read.com/SFG

www.ingramcontent.com/pod-product-compliance
Lightning Source LLC
Chambersburg PA
CBHW030358310726
48979CB00001B/348
9780975625507